A Broken Piece of the Puzzle and Other Stories

By Gabriel Gerometta and Jasmine Gauvin, and their Fellow Students

Deep Read Press

LAFAYETTE, TENNESSEE

deepreadpress@gmail.com

ISBN: 978-1-954989-64-1
Edited by: Brenda LeCrone Seaberg
Cover Design by: Kim Gammon
Cover Art by: Zoey Robinson
Title Page Art by: Raina Stoll
Published by:

Lafayette, Tennessee
www.deepreadpress.com
deepreadpress@gmail.com

Contents

Introduction

It takes a great deal of work to publish a book. For the seventh and eighth grade students who worked together to create this volume of short stories, the work began with their formulating and then refining story ideas and taking stock of the many things that make good stories—characters that are interesting, conflict that gets resolved (maybe), description that enhances instead of overpowers the text, etc. Then, those ideas were transformed into first drafts, which were revised again and again in response to the feedback received during numerous peer review sessions and at least one one-on-one session with me. Along the way, the students have learned about collaborating with others, managing their time, meeting deadlines, and expressing their creativity. To say that I am proud of them is an understatement.

–Deric McClard

A Broken Piece of the Puzzle

By Gabriel Gerometta and Jasmine Gauvin

Sarah Jones
Sept. 18, 2018

Today, I turned fifteen. I didn't get anything special, except for a cupcake from my friend Arthur. He is all I have had for a while. I'm happy because Arthur also gave me this journal that I am writing in. It's hard to believe, but it's been four years since my parents split.

Sept. 26, 2018

I almost forgot to write in my journal again haha. Stupid me. I realize I am not doing as well in school as I was. My mom hit me for it saying, "Get on with it!" She has been drinking again. This has been going on for months since Dad passed. I visited his grave again, and for the most part, it was tough, but someone has to move on. Even though my grades aren't what they should be, I still had a decent day. Arthur and I sat together at the lunch table and talked about hanging out after school for the first time ever. I'm pretty excited, but I guess I'll have to see how it goes.

Oct. 1, 2018

It is the beginning of October, finally. September was too long. Today is the day when I get to meet up with Arthur. He keeps joking that he has a three-story mansion; personally, I don't think that's true. I leave in about an hour from now, which is close to five. However, my mom would freak out if she found out that I was going to a boy's house. Wait, I know! I'll just say I'm going shopping for some groceries, and on my way home from Arthur's, I can grab a few things from the store. Perfect! I'm hoping my plan works.

Oct. 2, 2018

Last night was nice. Arthur and I hung out together, and he showed me his favorite hobbies, which include playing the guitar, photography, and some other things. My favorite has to be painting. I struggled to grasp all of this new information in the beginning, yes, but painting is more complex than I would've ever thought: putting colors in the right place, getting the proportions perfect, and some other important things I forgot. We painted lily pads and a pond. The experience created a sense of tranquility. The water painted on the canvas seemed to grow more real each minute with every swish of Arthur's brush.

Oct. 31, 2018

Today is most likely going to be the best day I'm going to have in a while. Arthur and I are going to a Halloween party tonight. It's difficult because I have to sneak out. There's no way my mother would let me go out to a party at night with a boy. It's worth it, though; Arthur and I are matching as vampires!

Oct. 31, 2018

I was caught. Yeah, this isn't the best scenario. Also, everything has been taken from me including my devices and all of the other things I love. It'll be ok, at least, I think.

I need self-improvement in my life. I need to turn things around and all.

The next morning, I woke up to the sound of the blaring of my alarm clock, and I began getting ready for school. It was a groggy and boring dawn, with my eyes barely able to stay open. I hurried out of my room and down the dimly lit hallway to eat something for breakfast. I did so quietly, being sure not to wake Mom. About seven minutes passed when I went along the sidewalk, walking several blocks to get to school. The breeze was ethereal and gentle; the birds chirped in the high canopy of the tree's branches. However, I was still about a quarter of a mile away from school.

Finally, I arrived while more students and a few teachers entered the building. It was chatty and loud with the general morning conversations. When I finally made it into the building, I saw Arthur beside our classroom entrance. Instantly, I felt my day get slightly better at the sight of my friend. I began to make my way over to him.

"Hey! You're early today," I greeted him.

"Yeah, my dad had to leave early, so he went ahead and dropped me off. I was waiting for you, though," he replied.

"That's cool," I replied dryly.

"Is something wrong? Did I do something to upset you?" he asked with a hurt expression on his face.

"Nothing," I said.

"What is it? Did something happen?" Arthur pushed hard for an answer.

"Mom figured out that I went to the party," I said apathetically. I just wanted to switch topics.

"How? You were so careful about everything. That *can't* be true, right?" he replied as he chuckled nervously.

"Yeah, that wasn't too fun to explain to my mom. I lost pretty much everything," I said as a nervous laugh also came out my mouth.

"I'm sorry," Arthur apologized sheepishly.

"It's fine, I could just sneak out again," I explicitly stated while taking a granola bar out of the bag I had grabbed before leaving my house.

"No!" he exclaimed.

"Why not?" I questioned while eating.

"Because you don't want to get into any more trouble, do you? Like, c'mon, don't you learn from your mistakes?" he asked.

"I do. I just don't care sometimes," I replied. "Anyways, we should go in before we get tardies."

"Yeah," he replied quietly.

We headed into the classroom for the first period as the school started to get more and more crowded. After everyone had entered the room, Mrs. Janice appeared. "Hello, Class. Today we will go over Pythagoras's theorem," she announced.

After setting up the White Board, she wrote, 'Thursday, November 1, 2018,' and began her lecture—a very boring one, indeed—when the lady whose voice often echoed through the intercom buzzed into our classroom.

"May I please have Sarah Jones come up to the office please? She's leaving," she stated.

"Have a good rest of your day Sarah," Mrs. Janice started. "Remember to turn in the homework tomorrow."

"Okay," I replied.

I made my way up to the office wondering why I would be picked up this early in the morning. As soon as I stepped out the first set of doors, I saw my mother sitting on the bench in the waiting area. She hadn't even noticed I had come in until I spoke up. This appeared strange to me. Then, I realized in horror she was probably intoxicated.

"What are you doing here, Mom? And why are you...umm, never mind. But that doesn't change the fact that it's not even nine in the morning yet," I said in an expectant tone.

"Let's go," she hiccupped.

"That didn't answer my question. What are you doing here?" I started to become exasperated.

"Calm down, Hun–"

"No, I won't calm down, Mom, and stop calling me Hunny– you know I hate that. Why are you here? If you don't answer me, I'm going back inside and will leave you out here to get home yourself. Plus, how did you not get pulled ov–"

"We're going to see your dad, Hun. He's cooked us dinner and everything," she said out of stupidity and intoxication.

"NO! Stop it, Mom. You need to get yourself together because Dad has been dead for months! You know what, I'm not even going to entertain you anymore because I am done playing your games. I'm going back inside. You have done nothing all these years except drink, cause me trouble, and ruin my life. You have been absent when I needed you most in my life! I will see you later," I said with resignation.

"Missy, you get over here at once before you're grounded longer!" she demanded.

I soon realized that the signs of her intoxication were wearing down. I went back into the school building in a rage, a fiery intense anger towards her. After slowly walking down the hallway, I looked back and didn't see her in the waiting room anymore, but that resentment still stuck. However, I tried to ignore it throughout the day; I shouldn't let it get to me.

Soon came lunchtime. I sat with Arthur, like usual, and talked about my next class: History. He looked at me with a concerned expression.

"Are you okay?" he asked.

I quickly regathered myself and replied, "O-oh yeah, I'm good."

"You sure? You seem...off."

"I'm positive," I insisted.

Some time passed before anything was said again. The lunchroom was quite lively, and the smell of pizza circulated through the air. Then, Arthur spoke again. "C'mon, I know for a fact that ain't true," he said.

"Like I just said, Arthur, I'm fine." I jokingly throw my packet of apples at him.

"Okay, I get it! Geez," Arthur laughed it off.

We continued eating lunch with the normal small talk like "How's your day been?" and "What did you do in this class?" Then, the lunch dismissal bell rang, and we went our separate ways for the day. I made it back to Room 307. After all of that, the lesson that lunch had interrupted commenced once again; the lecture was tedious. I just doodled the entire time and paid little attention to my teacher.

My teacher, Mrs. Jackson, began walking up to my desk to confront me. "Ms. Jones, is there something more important right now than paying attention to the lesson?" she asked firmly.

"No," I sheepishly replied, "I *was* paying attention."

"Alright then, when was the Proclamation Line put into place?" she questioned.

"Wait, I'm sorry, Miss, but could you tell me what that is again?" I asked, having completely forgotten what she had taught the previous day.

"That's enough to tell me that you, indeed, were not paying attention. To the principal's office...now!" she said sternly.

"But—"

"Now!" she repeated.

I finally got up out of my seat, my face flushed with red as every single one of my classmates looked at me. By the time I got out, I was crying. Tears flooded my eyes, and they stung. As I was walking to the office, I saw Arthur waiting outside the gym. He was sweating. I increased my pace as he looked at me. Then, I made it to the office. At that moment, I dried my face and entered, awaiting my punishment because of Mrs. Jackson.

The vice-principal took one look at me and said, "Again? You have been in my office about a million times since the beginning of the year." She sighed.

She then picked up the phone and called someone, but the sounds were unintelligible. I sat in the room for about thirty minutes when in the corner of my eyes, I saw the door open. Through the glass, I saw a woman. Her hair was bobbed and frizzy, and her nose was more pointed than a rapier. It was...my mother!

She grabbed my arm and dragged me to her car outside. She was silent, but her face showed a mess. She threw me in and began driving; I assumed she was taking me home. Soon, we arrived at our not so humble abode, and once we got inside, she slapped me with more force than she had ever used before.

"WHEN WILL YOU LEARN TO BEHAVE YOURSELF!" she exclaimed.

"I LITERALLY FORGOT ONLY ONE THING, MOM!"

"YOU'RE GROUNDED FOR LIFE!" she exclaimed again.

That time, I said nothing. Tears came to my eyes, but they didn't spill out. I closed my door and shut my eyes as I sat down, just thinking. Nothing. Then, I saw a paintbrush by my foot. I was intrigued. I remembered Arthur had forgotten it and never came back for it.

I picked it up and carefully inspected it between my fingers. It looked like it was made out of maple and had definitely had some usage. It had some paint dried on it with colors like light green, aquamarine, and some other indistinguishable colors whose names I didn't know.

Then, I saw a bunch of opened boxes with supplies in them under my bed and a note written on brown paper and folded in the shape of a paper airplane. It was from Arthur, and it read:

> *If you are reading this, you are probably bored or just good at finding things. Remember the time we painted together? Well, I had some extra supplies and wanted to donate them. I hope you enjoy the gift!*
> *– Your friend, Arthur*

"Hmm," I hummed in curiosity. "Wait, what? Did he just decide to just sneak in?!"

***

After my one-day suspension, I returned to school to ask Arthur why in the world he was in my house. Then, I saw him in front of the building.

"Hey! You're finally back!" he exclaimed.

"Hey!" I started, "I have a question for you."

"Yeah?"

"How in the world did you get into my house, Arthur!?"

"Umm, so you did find the note," he said sheepishly.

"Yeah. Soo...how'd you get into my house?" I asked again.

"I'm going to keep this explanation short, sweet, and simple; and let's just say I, um...snuck into your bedroom," he stated embarrassingly.

"W-What?!"

"I'm kidding," he started. "I disguised the supplies as boxed mail and had them on your front porch so that maybe, by some miracle, your mom would put them in your room."

"What about the note?" I asked suspiciously.

"Oh! I just folded it into a paper airplane and threw it through your open window," he explained.

"Oh," I said blankly.

"I'm sorry, I guess."

"It's fine."

"I hope you enjoy the donation."

"I will, thank you, but don't ever sneak into my bedroom again."

"Never said I would," he said in a sarcastic manner.

"We should go inside; class is about to begin," I stated.

"Wow, look at the time. Yeah, I agree; we should head in," he said in shock.

We both entered our first period. Mrs. Janice went up to the board and wrote the date: Monday, November 5, 2018. "Good morning," she said. "I hope you all had a good weekend. We will pick up where we left off on Monday."

"Pythagorean Theorem again? Really?" I said mostly to myself in frustration.

Mrs. Janice heard my remark but continued on anyway. It was a long and boring lesson that lasted the typical fifty minutes. Eventually, the second period came, then the third, then the fourth, then the fifth, and before I knew it, it was the end of the day.

I went to the auditorium to wait for my mother to pick me up. However, I sat there waiting and waiting until I was the last one left. Everyone else had been picked up. I was confused. I sat there for about thirty minutes before I decided just to walk home. I walked out the school building through the two metal doors after notifying the adults still there.

Then, rain began to fall, pitter-pattering on the sidewalk. The sidewalk grew darker as I continued walking. I started to increase my pace. Finally, I arrived at my doorstep and opened the door to see my mother lying lazily on the couch. She seemed drunk.

"Not again," I said facepalming myself, disappointed with her antics.

It was definitely something. I decided to go upstairs to my room and paint. I went through the supplies and found some paint, brushes, a canvas, and pencils. The only sounds that I heard were the air ventilation and my paintbrush against the paper.

A few hours later, I completed a somewhat decent realistic painting of an apple.

"Hmm," I thought to myself, "this can definitely use an improvement."

I threw it aside and decided to try again. Time after time I failed. Until my fiftieth try. I finally got a result I liked.

I decided to practice my art skills for a few weeks. Then, those weeks become months, the months become years, and before I knew it, I had graduated from art school. I began to think about my progress and a new dream that grew from my years of study.

"Am I even a good enough artist?" I asked myself.

***

I settled into an apartment roughly three hours from my mother's house and got a job at a nearby fast-food restaurant. I came home from my shift–it had been a really long day–and checked the mail. Since art school, I had wanted an opportunity somewhere just to reach me somehow. In the mailbox, I found a letter.

"Oh, what's this?" I asked. "Rent isn't due, I guess. I'll open it later."

I headed inside my apartment. It was fairly tidy with only a few items of clothing lying disorganized on the couch. The room had a familiar scent; it just felt like home.

I sat at the dining table with the letter in hand. I opened it with no expectations. Rip! I tore the seal on the envelope. "Oh, my goodness! No way!"

It was an art competition for the best of the best artists of our time. The person who wins would earn a total of $500,000. I was in shock. It was the opportunity I had been waiting for half of my life. I just couldn't turn the offer down.

The week before submission, I knew it was time to get to work. I began grabbing the various supplies I needed that range from pencils, brushes, paint, etc. I sat down at my workstation and began thinking, thinking about what to paint. The submission's theme had to be about nature. I sat there thinking about ideas. Nothing. Nothing, until about an hour later when I came up with something. A rose! Ah, yes, a good old rose. Simple, but sufficient.

Soon enough, I began. I made sure to add meaning to every brushstroke. Red, green, touches of yellow could be seen. The paint glided smoothly on the canvas and blended perfectly. Nevertheless, time worked like magic because finally, after five and a half hours, I was done.

***

Then, the day of submission finally arrived. I went to the building where submissions were dropped off and evaluated. It was about two hours away from where I lived. It was a pretty long drive, but soon, I was there. I walked in where I saw one of the hosts of the competition.

"Ah! Good evening…Ms. Dolores…is that right?" an official in the competition asked.

"Oh, yes, Ma'am," I replied.

We made small talk. Then, I gave her my piece, and she placed it on a desk. I left to return to my car but was stopped by a sign on the door. "Hosted by Arthur Brooke." The name sounded...familiar. Almost too familiar.

"Wait, is that... oh my!" I said, puzzled.

It was my old friend. This couldn't have been possible. It had to be a coincidence. I decided to put it off for the time being, figuring that he was probably greeting some guests. I just sat in my car during the judging. I was anxious. Maybe this was my chance to change my future. I would be able to join almost any art district.

After about an hour, time was up. I began getting ready to head back inside. I hopped out of the car and went to the building's bathroom, where I washed my face and tidied my clothes.

Three, two, one, and time! I made my way to the main room where the winner would soon be announced.

Someone tall and slim walked in the front of the crowd and announced, "Good evening, folks! I am glad everyone has gathered here tonight to announce the winner of the yearly art competition. I am Arthur Brook, the host of the event."

It suddenly became silent as the lights switched off.

"This year's art competition was a great one. It was hard to decide the winner, but we finally have a decision," he said. "The winner of this year's competition is...Dolores Jones!"

"Oh, my goodness! No, no, no, I'm dreaming right now," I said in complete shock and happiness.

Honestly, winning was great for me, but that $500,000 prize made it even better. I got to talk with Arthur a bit after the show to catch up on life. Also, he gave me something very important before I left.

"It was great talking to you, Dolores. I only wish you the best," he started. "Oh yes, I have something to give you. I've been holding on to it ever since graduation."

He gave me back my journal. All the memories came rushing back. It felt like I was experiencing high school all again, all in that one moment.

"Thank you," I said to him with sincere gratitude.

We parted ways for probably the last time, and I hopped into my car. I drove home and settled down. It was getting late, about 12:47. Finally, I went inside the bathroom to get ready for bed and relax after such a big achievement.

As I reclined in my bed, I wondered, *"Have I completed my part of the puzzle?"*

I Saw it All

By Abbey Carter

There are many things I remember from my teenage years: all the holidays I celebrated, my friends, and the crazy things we did. One of those crazy things ended up changing my life forever, and it still haunts me to this very day, October 31, 2024. It was the time I visited Cate's Cave.

It was twenty-five years ago, October 24, 1999, when my friends and I explored a cave. We got to Cate's Cave and started admiring all the rocks and geodes. Everything seemed alright for the longest time, and then, we went deeper into the cave.

Before we reached the entrance of the cave, there was a sign with big letters saying that there was NO RUNNING, NO JUMPING, OR ANYTHING LIKE THAT. If you did not follow those rules, you could be killed here. We all knew that. We'd been to the place too many times not to know that. When we arrived at the rocky part of the cave, Lexie's phone started ringing. She ignored it at first, then answered it when the calls did not stop for ten minutes. After what felt like the hundredth call, she picked up the phone. "OKAY, I'M COMING HOME RIGHT NOW!"

Lexie picked up her bag and started for the exit, jumping over all the rocks she could and stomping hard on the little ones. We felt everything start to shake when we heard a scream and a loud crash. We ran to see what had happened. I will never forget what we saw. Lexie was crushed underneath a huge rock, her phone lying beside her.

"LEXIE!" we yelled when we saw the splatter of blood everywhere, even on us.

"Lexie, what was that? Are you okay? ANSWER ME!" The sound of her mother's voice started to go quiet. We all ran to the phone. All we could say was "What happened to Lexie?" She would not listen to us, though, and the phone died.

We stayed there for a little while. We thought we needed to leave her, but we couldn't. Olivia was crying while we sat there. I still think about this and wonder how I remember it fully. Around what I think was twelve a.m., we took one last look at what Lexie had become and walked away. I tried to forget what I saw, but I couldn't. I saw it all.

We decided to look for the other exit. It was ten miles away. I grabbed everything of Lexie's that I could reach, everything not crushed by the rock. Olivia protested before we left the rock; she said it was inhumane to leave Lexie there. "OLIVIA! LEXIE'S GONE! THERE IS NOTHING WE CAN DO!" Olivia's boyfriend, James, yelled. Then, we began moving toward the exit.

After walking for maybe a mile, we entered a part of the cave we had never visited before. While we couldn't see anything, we could hear something crawling. James went exploring. He was trying to find where the noise was coming from. Then, we heard his screams.

We ran to find him, but it was too late. We saw his leg. That was the only thing we saw of him. We ran the other way, determined not to stop for anything. None of us cared if someone tripped. I started to run more and more slowly. Eventually, we all stopped running. We had been exerting ourselves for about a mile without stopping to rest. Hailey, Olivia, and I decided to stop for the night. With only three of us left, we slept for a while and then prepared to walk the rest of the eight miles.

Suddenly, Olivia realized that we had forgotten our supplies. "I think we left them behind when we started running," I said. Olivia agreed, but before we could say anything else, Hailey ran off.

She never stopped running. We chased her for about an hour until we caught up with her. The next thing I saw was Olivia launching at Hailey. I watched her jump on top of Hailey and start to beat her up for abandoning us like that. I had to pull them off each other. After we caught our breath, we decided to stop again for the night and talk about what had happened. Hailey said she had seen a snake and ran to avoid it, but Olivia and I both knew she was lying. I went to sleep just to get a break from the day. By this point, we had five miles left till the exit.

***

I woke up the next morning to find that Hailey was missing again. Olivia wouldn't tell me where Hailey was, so I had to look for her myself. I eventually found her–what was left of her, that is–but she was not the happy, loving, sweet, kind, caring person I knew. All I found was her lifeless body. She was the one person I had left to keep me from going crazy, and she was gone.

It was hard to keep walking with Olivia because she didn't talk much, but when she did, all she talked about was her boyfriend and how much she missed him. I was tired of listening to her complaints and finally lost it. "I DO NOT CARE! YOU JUST KILLED THE ONLY PERSON I HAVE EVER HAD BY MY SIDE SINCE I MOVED HERE!"

"BUT I LOVED HIM, AND HE WAS THE ONLY ONE WHO EVER GAVE THE SAME AMOUNT OF LOVE BACK!" I left the conversation at that. I couldn't talk anymore about this situation. Hailey, James, Lexie–they were all gone and never coming back. I missed them so much. I wished they hadn't had to die. Lexie hadn't deserved that, Hailey had done nothing, and we didn't know what had happened to James. Why did they have to go? Why couldn't it have been Olivia? Why couldn't it have been me? I didn't want to live with this guilt. I saw it all happen.

I wanted to go home. I was done with that awful cave. It had taken everything from me: my friends, my family, sports, everything. Olivia and I stopped for the night, and when I woke up, something felt different. Olivia was gone. I had no idea what had happened to her. I had to keep walking, though, for Lexie, James, and Hailey. For all I cared, Olivia could stay down there in the cave forever. The whole time I had been trying to escape from this awful cave, I had grabbed something belonging to each person when they had died: Lexie's dead phone, Hailey's basketball bracelet, and James' anklet. Before I began the final mile, I turned around. I had to get something of Olivia's. Even if I hated her, I had to come up with something for her family. I took her earrings, the large silver hoops she always wore. She had left them behind. With Olivia's earrings in hand, I began the last mile. I didn't want to stay in this cave any longer. I'd seen too much down here. I saw it all.

That final mile was awful. I was all alone, but I kept walking. Just before seeing the light of the outside world, I felt that I couldn't leave. I couldn't leave everyone behind. My heart was broken. I had to continue, though. No way could I stay here after all I had been through. Then, I saw the sun, the grass, and the bright blue sky. I made it out. All around the cave were police officers who had been trying to find us. Everyone's parents were there to pick them up. When I walked out, everyone started gathering around me. My parents followed. The other parents were yelling at me. I got pulled away by the police and stayed in the hospital for a couple of days.

When I was in the hospital, many police officers questioned me. For a while, they tried to say I had killed my friends. Nothing ever came of it, though, because they couldn't find any evidence to support their claims. When I was finally released from the hospital, I went back home and tried to forget about everything that happened. I never did, though. I couldn't. I will always remember what happened that night, October 24, 1999, when my friends and I began exploring Cate's Cave.

The Halloween Party

By Haidyn Carver and Westyn Carver

At first, Luke Osborn seemed like a nice and gentle guy until Stacy Jane saw the true side of him. Stacy and Luke seemed like a fine and happy couple at first, and they were, but after a while, he started being rude, and became furious if she talked to other boys. He screamed at her, and sometimes, he even hit her if he saw her talking with them. She went to school and told her friends, and they said she should break up with him, but she never listened because she was too scared. One day, something changed in her, and she finally took their advice and broke up with Luke.

As she expected, it did not turn out well. After she said that she wanted to break up with him, he started screaming at her and trying to hit her while not letting her leave the house. She called her friend Windy Geralds and told her what was happening. Windy asked her brother Bentley to help get her out of the house, so he helped Windy rescue Stacy. Windy knocked on the door to distract Luke while Bentley helped Stacy crawl out the window. Then, he and Stacy started hanging out with each other a lot. Eventually, they started dating. Luke found out and tried to do something about it because he was still in love with Stacy. He came up with a plan. He knew that as Halloween approached, Stacy would invite the whole school to her house for a big Halloween party, like she did every year. Luke planned to go.

During the party, Windy discovered a dead body in the bathroom. Everybody became terrified and left the house except Stacy, Bentley, Windy, and their friends Karlee Ross and Kenzie Brook. Luke also stayed, but nobody knew he was in the house. Everybody in the house stayed together. After a while, nothing happened, so they decided to split up into groups, but they would all still stay alert. Stacy, Bentley, and Kenzie stayed together in one group while Windy and Karlee were in another. They started cleaning up after the party. Suddenly, Stacy heard a loud noise. It sounded like glass shattering. A few seconds later, Karlee came running down the hall screaming and crying. She had blood all over her and cuts on her arms and legs. The others were terrified and ran to her. They asked what had happened and where Windy was. Karlee said, "The killer! It was the killer! He came out of nowhere and stabbed her. I ran to her and picked her up, but she was already dead; then, he started chasing after me. He cut my arms and legs with the knife he had used to kill Windy, but I was faster than he was. I got away." Everyone had started crying but Bentley. It was harder for him to accept because Windy was his sister and they had a really strong bond with each other.

Stacy and Kenzie cleaned up Karlee's cuts and decided to call the police. However, they had taken so many pictures and watched so many videos during the party that their phones were dead. Except Stacy's. But it was upstairs in her room charging because it had died in the middle of the party. Everyone went upstairs together. They thought the killer would not attack them if they stayed together.

Suddenly, they heard a noise. They were scared and ran to Stacy's bedroom. What they didn't know was that it was just Luke, not the killer as they suspected. Bentley and Stacy decided to check it out and found Luke hiding in the master bedroom. They brought him back into Stacy's room, but then they found that Kenzie was dead. Karlee was not in the room, either. Overcome by fear, they started searching for Karlee, but they could not find her. Then, they started thinking that Karlee might be the killer because every time they left someone alone with her, that person always died. Also, they did not know that Karlee had been watching them the whole time, and when they figured it out, she jumped out and attacked Stacy. She held Stacy with a knife against her neck and told the boys to get back or she would kill Stacy. Stacy was crying and said, "Why are you doing this to me? I thought we were friends."

Karlee said, "Because you stole Luke from me. He was supposed to be mine. He was supposed to date me, not you. He chose you even though he had known me longer. You knew that I liked him."

Then, Stacy said, "I asked you if it was ok if I dated him, and you said yes. If you had a problem with it, you should have just told me and I never would have dated him. You were so supportive when I told you what he was doing to me."

Karlee said, "That's why I told you to break up with him; then, this never would have happened."

The boys looked at each other and nodded like they could read each other's mind while Stacy and Karlee were arguing. Karlee saw them and told them not to try anything, or she would kill Stacy. She did not want to because she really wanted to torture Stacy before she killed her just like Stacy had tortured her feelings. As Karlee started backing up, she took Stacy to a guest bedroom and locked the door so nobody could get in. The room had a window, but it was locked, and Luke and Bentley would need a ladder to reach it from the outside. Somehow, they had to figure out how to free Stacy without being caught. They made a plan. They would bring a crowbar with them as they climbed up the ladder from Stacy's garage. Then, they would smash the window and hop in, knock Karlee out, and save Stacy.

This proved to be easier said than done. While they were outside looking for the crowbar and setting up the ladder, Karlee was torturing Stacy. She punched her in the face and cut her arms and legs. Then, Bentley and Luke heard Stacy scream, so they decided to give up on the crowbar and started climbing up the ladder. They broke the window with their fists. When they entered the guest room, Stacy was dead, and Karlee was nowhere to be found. The police search continued for years, but they never found her. Luke and Bentley never gave up looking for her, either.

Wolf in Sheep's Clothing

by Kiera Dyer

[RING...RING...]
[PLEASE LEAVE A MESSAGE AFTER THE BEEP. *BEEP*]
James?! It's Sara; she's terribly injured! Call me back as soon as you can! Please!

***

"I call my first witness, Aaron Simpson," the prosecutor said to Judge Butch Wilson as Aaron Simpson took the stand. Aaron was twenty-three and had been dating Sara Watson, a twenty-one-year-old girl who was injured heavily and hospitalized. Aaron had short, brown hair and was known to be quite the charmer. Sara had short, blonde, straight hair that came to her shoulders, and was also known to be very pretty. She was a victim of attempted murder and the daughter of James Watson, a good friend of Judge Butch's.

"Mr. Simpson, you have been accused of the attempted murder of Mr. Watson's daughter, Sara Watson. How do you plead?" Judge Butch said to Aaron.

"Not guilty," Aaron replied, staring daggers into the judge's eyes.

"What is your testimony?" the prosecutor asked as everyone in the courtroom turned to Aaron.

He didn't look away from the lawyer as he spoke: "I took her out for coffee the other day. Haven't seen her since. She texted me the day after and told me she was going to the park to study with her brother Jason." Jason Watson was Sara's older brother, the son of James Watson. He was known for being a little off—no, *very* off. He never really talked to anyone, and whenever he actually spoke to anyone, he was usually cold and mean. He was a weird guy.

"When did she text you, Mr. Simpson?" the prosecutor asked.

"Wednesday, the day she was found," Aaron replied, sounding a little too casual.

"So, you took her out for coffee Tuesday?" the prosecutor asked, just to be sure.

"Yes, sir," Aaron confirmed.

The prosecutor spoke once more. "Thank you. Your Honor, no further questions."

Judge Butch spoke up. "The defense may now cross examine the witness."

Aaron looked over at the defendant.

"Did you see her at all after she texted you?" the prosecutor said.

"No, sir," Aaron replied.

The Prosecutor nodded. "Thank you. Your Honor, no further questions."

Judge Butch spoke. "You may step down. Prosecution, you may call your second witness."

"Thank you, Your Honor. I call Jason Watson to the stand," the prosecutor said as Jason stepped up to the podium, his right hand scratching at his left arm. Jason had always been off. He had short, black hair that covered his face, and he wore a black hoodie with the hood pulled up over his head. He had big, dark brown eyes, and he always tilted his head down so it looked like he was

26

glaring at you. He always scratched at his left arm when stressed or angry, almost to the point of breaking skin. It was nearly impossible to tell that he was Sara's brother.

"Mr. Watson, Mr. Simpson just told us that Sara hung out with you on Wednesday. Is that correct?" the prosecutor asked him.

"Yes, sir," Jason replied, his voice deep and raspy as always. He stared directly into the judge's eyes, not blinking once.

"And what did you two do?" the prosecutor asked.

"We went to the park to study and talk." Both Sara and Jason were in college. Jason scratched at his arm a little more aggressively, his expression showing no sign of pain at all.

"That is all you did?" the prosecutor continued.

"Yes, sir. She said she was thinking about breaking up with Aaron. I asked her why, and she said she just wasn't happy with their relationship. That's all she said. She stopped by the wine shop before she went home, but I didn't think anything of it. I heard about her injuries later that day."

The prosecutor asked, "Why were you not home, Mr. Watson?"

"She left early while I stayed in the park to study some more," Jason replied.

The prosecutor spoke again: "Thank you, Your Honor, no further questions."

Judge Butch nodded and said, "The defense may cross-examine the witness."

The defense attorney spoke. "How did you hear about her injuries, Mr. Watson?"

"Our mother told me about them. Said my sister was going to be in the hospital for a while," Jason replied.

"Thank you, Your Honor, no further questions," the defense attorney said.

Judge Butch nodded. "You may step down. Court is adjourned until 10 a.m. tomorrow," he said as he slammed his gavel down twice, dismissing everyone.

***

"You really think my son did this to his own sister?" Mary Watson, the mother of both Jason and Sara and the spouse of

Butch Watson, asked Aaron as they stood just outside the courthouse.

"As much as I hate to say it, it's certainly a possibility. He was the one who was last with her," Aaron replied.

Mary sniffed and wiped a tear from her eye, still in disbelief that her son may have hurt her daughter. Her daughter lying in the hospital after being terribly injured was already bad enough, and the thought that her own son did this was like salt in an open wound. "I just don't believe it. Jason wouldn't hurt a fly."

Aaron knew that he probably would if he got the chance, but he didn't want to say that to Jason's mother. "Only time will tell who hurt her," Aaron suggested. "I'm going to check up on her at the hospital, just to see how she's doing."

***

Aaron drove to the hospital and walked into Sara's hospital room. He was wearing his favorite black hoodie with the hood pulled up over his head. "Jesus..." he mumbled to himself when he saw Sara. Her throat had been slit with some kind of sharp object, and she was covered in bruises and cuts. The heart monitor next to her bed continuously beeped, telling him she was alive.

"I know. It's sickening to think someone would do this to such a sweet and kind girl." Aaron jumped slightly at the voice and turned around quickly. It was Sara's nurse, Mrs. Emily. Mrs. Emily was about thirty years old and had long, blonde hair up in a ponytail and wore a face mask. She spoke with a soft voice, "Apologies for startling you, Mr...."

"Simpson. Aaron Simpson."

The nurse nodded and smiled behind her face mask. "Nice to meet you, Mr. Simpson. I'm Mrs. Emily. Mrs. Emily Williams. I'm Sara's nurse," she said as she held out her hand to shake. Aaron took it, shaking it gently with a smile.

"Are you related to Sara?" Mrs. Emily asked Aaron.

"No, I'm her boyfriend," he replied.

"Oh, okay," she nodded as she spoke. She opened her mouth to speak again, but the buzz of the intercom filled the room, interrupting her.

The sound of Mrs. Emily's boss' voice said, "MRS. EMILY, COME TO THE LOBBY, PLEASE. MRS. EMILY, COME TO THE LOBBY."

"Oh, I have to go. I'll probably be gone for just a second. I trust you'll be alright with her in here?" Mrs. Emily said to Aaron as she stood next to the door.

"Yeah, I'll be fine," he replied. She smiled behind her face mask again and left the room without saying another word.

Aaron went over to Sara's bed and looked down at her. Her eyes were closed, almost as if she were dead, but the beeping heart monitor proved she was still alive. Aaron scowled down at her and spoke under his breath, "Just another wolf in sheep's clothing..."

***

The next day, Aaron woke up to his phone ringing. He sat up, stretched, yawned, and answered the phone. "Hello?" he said, his voice strained from just waking up. He heard Mary's frantic voice on the other end.

"Aaron?! Aaron, Sara's dead!"

"What?!" he replied immediately.

"Her heart monitor flatlined last night! Come to the hospital, now!" she yelled, sounding both scared and confused and ready to cry at any minute.

Aaron showed up at the hospital to see two men carrying her body out of the hospital. Mary ran out of the hospital, crying. She walked quickly over to Aaron, speaking in between sobs. "I don't believe this. They found her life support unplugged this morning. Someone must've done this last night."

"You think it was the nurse?" Aaron asked.

"No, she took the rest of the day off yesterday. Her daughter started throwing up," Mary replied.

So that's why she was called to the lobby, Aaron thought. "I think Jason said something about going to see her. Maybe he did it," he lied.

"Y-you really think so?" Mary's voice broke as she continued to sob. "I can't believe this. I'll get the police to check the cameras."

29

***

Judge Butch slammed his gavel. "The trial of Jason Watson will now come to order. Mr. Watson, did you murder your sister, Sara Watson?"

Jason looked around with his cold stare, taking in every single person in the courtroom, then stared the judge right in the eyes and said, "No, Your Honor."

"The police checked the cameras. They found a man wearing a black hoodie with the hood pulled over his head unplugging her life support after Mrs. Emily left."

"Fine, I confess. I killed her," Jason declared, his hand going back to clawing at his arm again.

Aaron's eyes widened slightly, but he forced himself to stay calm. He knew Jason didn't do this, and he also knew that most likely nobody would believe him if he said so.

The judge responded, "You are to spend no fewer than fifteen years in prison. Court adjourned." The judge slammed the gavel down, dismissing everyone.

***

Aaron attended Sara's funeral, along with James and Mary Watson. He watched as Sara was buried, his expression blank. After the funeral, both he and Mary went to Sara's room to collect all of her things. Mary swore she saw something glistening under Sara's bed, but she didn't mention it. She thought it was probably a piece of glass or jewelry or something like that. She looked over at Sara's desk and saw an empty bottle of alcohol. She picked it up and examined it closely. Red wine. "Was this Sara's?" she mumbled quietly and wiped her eye. "I can't believe that Jason did this. I just can't believe it." she spoke out loud again.

"I can't either," Aaron agreed in a somewhat dark tone. "But Sara deserved it. She was just a wolf in sheep's clothing."

Mary looked up at him in slight disbelief. "What do you mean?" she asked.

Aaron got on his knees and reached under Sara's bed, pulling out a knife. A huge knife with blood stains on the tip of the blade. Mary's eyes widened at the sight of it. "I-is that a—"

"Yes, it is," Aaron interrupted. "I never took her out for coffee Tuesday. I invited her, but she said she was busy. She called me Wednesday after she had studied with Jason and told me to come to her room so we could talk." He looked down at the knife and ran his index finger over the blood stains as he spoke: "I came to her room, and she looked and sounded drunk, nothing like when she called me. That's when I saw the empty bottle. She cursed at me, saying she had always hated me, then said she'd always wanted to kill me."

Aaron moved his hand to his sleeve and pulled it up, showing a huge, deep cut on his arm and other tiny cuts. Mary covered her mouth in disbelief. "She pulled the knife out from under her bed and got a good hit on me. I wrestled her for the knife and eventually tore it out of her grasp, then she started screaming for help." Aaron smiled like a maniac: "So I got rid of her."

The words echoed in Mary's mind. She backed up slowly against the wall and mumbled behind her hand, "Y-you're a liar...you're a monster..."

Aaron just laughed and stepped closer. "That incident taught me something; no one's perfect, everyone is a wolf in sheep's clothing, no matter how innocent they appear." He stepped even closer to her as he continued, "So just be extra careful in your next life." He raised the knife as Mary trembled in fear. "And pray that God is really as kind and merciful as he appears to be when you see him."

***

[RING...RING...]
[PLEASE LEAVE A MESSAGE AFTER THE BEEP. *BEEP*]
Mr. Watson, it's Aaron! Your wife, Mary, she's dead!

I am Sorry

By Camden Russell and Hunter Farley

"Good morning, Daddy!" my four-year-old daughter said.

"Good morning, Sweetie," I replied. I had just woken up from sleeping after spending many hours at work. My wife, Jessie, and my daughter, Taylor, are everything to me.

"Zach," Jessie said, "what do you want for breakfast?"

"Hmm, probably some scrambled eggs with pancakes."

"YES! PANCAKES!" Taylor screamed, nearly bursting my eardrums.

"Taylor, Honey, not so loud," Jessie told her.

"Sorry," said Taylor.

A few minutes later, we finished breakfast.

"I'm off to work," I told Jessie.

"I love you, Zach," Jessie said to me.

"I love you both, too," I told them, wrapping them in a hug. I headed out the door to go to work. I had a new case. More than two counts of manslaughter. I worked on it all day; then, I received a text message from my friends.

THE BOYS

(Morgan)
Yo, are we heading to the bar tonight?

(Zach)
Fine by me

(Weston)
I'll be there

***

I made it home to eat supper, then told my wife I was going to the bar. "That's fine, but don't drive home." I told her I wouldn't. I got in my car and left. I made it to the bar, met up with my friends, and got a couple of drinks. Soon, we began talking about life.

"I've got a new house and a nice Mercedes," Morgan told us.

"I have a new house, too," Weston replied.

"What do you have, Zach?" Weston and Morgan asked in unison.

"I do not have much, but I have my wife and daughter, and they are my everything."

"Oh...okay," Weston told me.

"That's nice, I guess," Morgan added.

Realizing my friends cared more about money than what really matters in this world made me sad. This caused me to drink even more, which made me feel off, but I did not stop. When I couldn't take any more alcohol, I paid and hobbled to my car. I started to drive home and was off to a good start. I was stopping at red lights and going on green lights, but then I made it to the highway.

I was getting tired and trying to keep myself from passing out. I was struggling to stay conscious while swerving between lanes and dodging cars. Then, my eyes closed, and before passing out, I heard a crash.

I woke up. My vision was blurry, and I had a loud ringing in my ears. I couldn't feel my legs, and my back was killing me. Then, everything went black.

***

I woke up when I heard someone calling me on my phone. It was a co-worker, another detective, so I answered. "Hello?"

"Hey, Zach. It's me, Cody. We have a new case, and I know legally you cannot be involved, but I could use your help."

"Why can't I be involved? Is it because of the nature of the crime or the parties involved?" I asked.

"Uh...it's about the people. Your wife and daughter were killed in a car accident," he said in a sad tone, "and we need to figure out what happened and whose fault it was–whether it was your wife or Jackson Lee, the man we used to go to school with," Cody answered.

"Okay, I will call you later," I told him just before hanging up. I started to cry, and I wanted to know who killed them.

***

As soon as I got out of bed, I rushed to the office. I opened the door, only to find the analysis of the case on my desk. I was reading the case when I remembered playing around the house with my daughter and laughing with my wife. I wished that I could just go back in time to save them. I teared up again, and my teardrops landed on the paper.

"Zach, we need to go out to the scene of the accident to look at the wrecked cars and examine the corpses," Cody told me.

"I'll take the cars," I replied, shaken by his words.

When we arrived at the scene of the accident, I looked at the demolished vehicles. Jessie drove an old Ram 1500, and Jackson Lee was in a new Nissan truck. The truck's bottom was badly damaged, but where he was sitting was barely scratched. However, Jessie's truck was totaled. It was sickening to think about the pain they had endured. I clocked out so I could clear my mind.

***

When I went home, I went straight to bed. I needed a nap to relieve my stress. I couldn't go to sleep for about forty-five minutes, but then, when I woke, I wasn't in my room. I was in my office, but no one else was there. "Hello?" I yelled. "Hello?"

I walked out of the office into the main lobby; still, no one was there. Then, I heard a whisper: "It's all your fault." Goosebumps shot down my spine; it was bone-chilling.

I went to check out the upstairs, following the voice that kept repeating, "It's all your fault." I drew closer to the voice. Then, a door flew open. I heard footsteps. A little girl walked out of the room, but it wasn't an ordinary girl; it was a girl who looked just like she had risen from the grave. The girl continued to say, "It's all your fault," but then she screamed, "IT'S ALL YOUR FAULT, ZACH!" Then, I woke up in my room. I was so pale and sweaty. I'd apparently had a nightmare. I needed time to process what had happened.

A few minutes later, I jumped out of bed and drove to work. I was working on a homicide case, and while analyzing the crime scene, I slipped and hurt my arm. Cody took me to the hospital. "What happened, Doctor?" I asked.

"You broke your wrist," he replied.

"Dang, I will take you home so you can relax for a bit," Cody told me. I hated being at home ever since my family died, but I agreed simply to avoid an argument.

The doctor had wrapped my wrist and said we were okay to leave. As we were walking down the hallway, I noticed something. There was a guy sitting in the hallway with a cast on his arm. He seemed familiar for some reason, but I could not place him. "Where have I seen that guy before?" I whispered to myself.

"Mr. Jackson Lee, come into my office," a doctor said. It was Jackson Lee! His pale, blue eyes stared at me. My emotions overwhelmed me. I wanted to hurt him for everything he had done to me.

***

A few days went by. A plan was forming in my mind, and it was perfect. Jackson used to work at a restaurant with me, but now he owned it. So, I decided to eat there, ask for the manager, and shoot him so I could get revenge for Jessie and Taylor. I had to be lucky enough to find him because he owned multiple restaurants.

I walked into his pizza place called Jack's Pizza right before it closed for the night and ordered a cheese pizza and a Coke so I didn't seem suspicious. Then, I asked the waitress, "Can I see the manager? I want to give him a donation for his charity, and I want a photo with him."

"Oh, he will be so delighted!" the waitress said in awe. He walked over to me, we took the photo, and right before I shook his hand, I pulled the gun out. I pointed it and pulled the trigger. BANG! Everything went black.

***

B*eep! Beep! Beep!* I heard a machine. Opening my eyes, I could see bright lights. "Where am I?" I murmured to myself.

"Sir, calm down, you just woke up from a coma; everything is alright," the doctor told me.

"Where's my wife? Where is Taylor? I want to see them," I said with tears in my eyes.

"Um, they're in a better place now, Sir."

"What do you mean?"

When the doctor was about to answer my question, I heard it again. The whisper. The little girl from my dream. "It's all your fault, Dad," the girl said.

"What?" I whispered to myself. "No, it can't be."

"You are the reason we are not alive, Dad," the girl said. "You killed me and Mom. I will never forgive you."

At that moment, I realized the girl I was speaking to was Taylor, my daughter. Then, I heard the doctor say, "You got into a car crash with your wife and daughter, but they were in the other vehicle. Your truck destroyed their car. They. Had. No. Hope," the doctor told me.

***

When they released me from the hospital, I was arrested on two counts of manslaughter and a DUI. I was put in prison, and a few weeks later, it was time for my trial.

"Order in the court," the judge said. "Mr. Zachary Kennedy Lee, you are charged with two counts of manslaughter and a DUI." I knew I was not going to get out of this, but my lawyer tried anyway.

"Not Guilty, Your Honor." I hung my head in shame and started to tear up again.

"Bring up your first witness, Prosecutors," the judge said.

Then, I saw him. "Part-Time Officer Jackson Lee," one of the prosecutors said, "did you see your brother, his wife, and their daughter in the crash?"

"Yes," Jackson told the man. At that moment, I remembered he was my brother.

"Which vehicle was on the wrong side: Jessie's or Zach's?" the prosecutor asked.

"Zach was on the wrong side," he told him.

"No further questions, Your Honor."

I knew there was no escaping this. Even if I was not guilty, I would still have to live the rest of my life knowing that I killed my wife and daughter. As the trial continued, I just sat there, wishing this would be over. Finally, the jury came back with their verdict.

"Have you reached a verdict?" the judge asked.

"We have, your honor. We find the defendant guilty," the foreman announced.

"Mr. Zachary Kennedy Lee, I hereby sentence you to thirty-six years in prison, and you will not be eligible for parole until year twenty-four. Court adjourned," the judge declared.

I sat there in silence, unable to speak.

The officers took me to my cell. I couldn't do anything but cry. My daughter's face haunted me. I could only tell by her voice it was Taylor, because her body was so messed up. Her face was badly decomposed. Her pale, blue eyes were white. I could not believe what I had done. My disbelief and shame grew so great that I began to bawl. I was allowed to give my loved ones a funeral and even to attend, but I did not have enough money. Not enough to buy two caskets, so I decided to have them cremated. The only words that I was able to say were, "I am sorry." The only image I had in my head was the wording on the tombstone:

Jessie and Taylor Lee, wife and daughter of Zach Lee, taken by fate.

My Forever Trip to Canada

By Isabelle Nash and Izabella Felts

Journal of Sarah Olivia Bell

Prologue

I never liked my parents, neither when they were together nor when they were apart. My dad abused me and my mom, turning her into a drug addict. Her drug abuse worsened after my father threatened to take custody of me after they split nine years ago. I have been switching between houses ever since. Although I do remember a girl – my sister - that I used to travel with, I haven't seen her in many years. I have to deal with something new every minute.

When I'm at my mom's house, I have to clean the mess caused by her addiction. Once when she was high and I was cleaning, I murmured, "I wish you weren't my mother." I guess being on drugs heightens people's senses because she started yelling at me. The words "I wish I had kept your twin instead" pierced through my soul. All went quiet after those mistaken words were said. I loved my sister. I had always thought that she had abandoned me. The fact that my mom knew why she disappeared from my life and that she may have been the cause of that disappearance was surprising news to me. I asked her what she meant, but she just sat on the couch in silence. I begged her to tell me. Instead, she kept getting angrier. The rage built up so much that in an instant I was pushed to the wall and my mom threatened to shave my head completely. Total baldness. I replied both in anger and sadness, "Maybe I'll just leave on my own, but I can't because YOU WILL BE LOST WITHOUT ME!" She was shocked at my response but yelled at me once more to go to my room. I gladly turned my back to my opponent and slowly walked to my room. Not in defeat but in determination to make a change in my cursed life.

My father's house is only slightly worse. At his house, I get new things thrown at me every day, literally. An incident happened once when I was little and didn't understand that getting things thrown at me was wrong. My father threw an ashtray at my head, and it shattered on contact. I still have a dinosaur-shaped scar on my forehead.

I have been babysitting my parents since they split. This has all become too much for me. I can't take the stress of life anymore.

May 2, 2017

Now, I'm here. Sitting on my bed with my bags packed, ready to restart this life. Where will I go? No idea. Where will I live? Not a clue. How will I get there? Over my head. Who will I be? My plan is anyone but Sarah Olivia Bell. There are a lot of undecided factors to my proposal, but whatever happens, I would rather be there than here.

A few hours have passed, and I'm still sitting here with my bags, wondering what to do. I peek into the living room. It looks like more chaos for me to clean. If I stick with my plan, I won't be here long enough to clean the clutter once she awakes from her drug-induced sleep. I hope to be gone by morning.

My window is open, and my mom is asleep. The perfect time to leave. I have exactly ten dollars, enough to get two bus tickets, just in case I need to go farther than planned.

May 3, 2017

I am on the bus. There are few people due to the fact it is 12:30 in the morning on a Tuesday. I have made a friend: Edna. From what I've been told, she came from a poor family like me. She looks to be in her early 50s and is very sweet. I asked her why she was on the bus at this early hour. She said she was headed home from work. I understand very well why she wouldn't want to work any earlier: The traffic is bizarre. While my and Edna's conversations have been nice, it is time for me to continue my journey to a better life.

It is around 4 A.M now, and I am on a bench outside of a Starbucks. I can see the dew on my pen. Somehow, I ended up in Ontario, Canada. Far from home in Chicago. I'm clueless as to what I'm going to do next.

I can see a beautiful lady on the bench across the street, I may ask her for help. Or possibly the homeless man who has been digging in the trash on and off for the past twenty minutes. I introduced myself and asked her if she could help me. Her name is Amelia Bell. How ironic. She had my last name. Name of the sister which my mom sent away. She is exactly how I remember her. Is this my sister? Have I finally found her?

May 17, 2017

It has been two weeks, and I live in a homeless shelter for the abused. Amelia Bell, the girl from the streets, and I are working to find and imprison my parents. She seemed shocked when I told her their names, almost like a memory had come to light. She showed me a scar caused by her father. As she lifted the sleeve of her coat, I saw a birthmark. The same as mine. I have put the pieces together. She looks almost identical to me. She knew the awful people whom I called my parents. As she lifted the sleeve of her coat, I saw a birthmark. The same as mine. I have put the pieces together. Could it be that she is my sister? Have I finally found her? The statement "I think you're my sister" seemed awkward to say at the time, given the fact we had only just gotten to know each other. She asked if I had siblings. She needed to know if there was anyone else being harmed. I told her my sister got sent away and left me behind to deal with my mother on my own. She asked my sister's name, and I told her Amelia. She told me she got sent away and had to leave her sister behind. We both made the connections. She is my sister! I'm not completely alone!

May 31, 2017

Amelia and I have been living in her house for two weeks, planning a way to get back at our parents for everything they had done to us. We knew our parents would not have wanted us to reunite, for we would take them down. Do we care about their opinions? No. Not really.

June 7, 2017

I love living with my sister. We got a dog! He is a brown Labrador named Charlie (Charlie Brown), I have my own room, and we are going to the mall to get me a new wardrobe today. My life is looking up. I am so much happier here with my sister and Charlie.

Anytime I hear my name said in a remotely loud tone, I have flashbacks of my parents calling out to me. I could not stand it anymore, so I legally changed my name to Olive Bell. As Olive Bell, I have never been abused or abandoned.

June 14, 2017

Never did I think I would have a dog and live without my parents. Neither of them liked animals, so the closest things I had to a pet were the birds in the cornfield across the street. However, if I had tried to pick up a bird, it would have attempted to peck my eye out. If I try to pick up Charlie, he lays in my arms as if I am the bed he sleeps in. Being without my parents has been peaceful. Not having projectiles thrown at my face reassures me that I made the right decision.

June 20, 2017

I have figured out what I want to do with my life and gotten a head start. My sister has been working as a Child Protective Services agent for two years, and that is my dream job. My parents always put on a fake smile, so I never asked for help. I will regret that for the rest of my life. If anyone asked me about a bruise, I told them I fell down the stairs. For the dinosaur scar, I tell people I fell on a rock. Every call we get, I am thankful these children have the courage to ask for help. Other calls, I'm not so thankful for. Sometimes we get calls from schools, or friends with suspicions. I get mad at myself for allowing things to get this bad. I know this isn't my fault, but deep down I think of reasons to believe it is.

Helping these children is my passion. Just last week, Amelia and I went to a house to check in, and one of the little girls ran out and hugged my waist as she asked for help. Her name was Jesse, and I knew I had to help her. We could visibly tell she needed help. She looked malnourished and sleep-deprived. We found her a foster home with a really nice family. The parents have talked to us about a forever-adoption. Moments like these are what make me love my job.

July 1, 2017

I'm buying a house! I found a two-story not that far from my sister. I have been saving money for a while, and I can finally afford it. Amelia offered to pitch in and help, but I denied the offer. She found me a place to work when I needed it. She offered me support when I was alone. She gave me a home when I was homeless. It would be too much to ask her to help me buy my home when I am more than capable of doing it myself.

July 4, 2017

Happy Fourth of July! Amelia and I are hosting a party at my new house. We are using my house because it has a pool. We got over three hundred dollars worth of fireworks. This day is going to be extra special because it will mark the first holiday in my new life as Olive Bell. We are inviting some of her friends as well as the friends I made at the shelter. Now that I think about it, this is the first party I have ever thrown, mostly because my mom was too much of a drug addict for any of my friends at school to come to our home. She didn't like any noise other than the noise she caused.

The party started about thirty minutes ago, and everyone is already here. I had to sneak away while no one was paying any attention. Now that I think about it, I didn't even have to. I have been splashed about five times in the past five minutes. For my first party, it isn't as crazy as I imagined.

April 17, 2021

It has been a few years since I have written in you. I'm not sure when I lost you, but from what I've read, it was after the Fourth of July party four years ago. A lot has changed since then. I have a beautiful daughter, Jade, and a loving husband, Dylan Larusso. My daughter is three years old and I would never treat her the way my parents treated me. Charlie Brown moved from my sister's house to mine, and I think he was happy with that change. However, the most exciting part is that we got our parents into rehab! We will never be able to forgive them, but we are trying to make them better people. I know no one can be too old to have a journal, but it's time to retire you. You have been good to me, and you know all of my secrets. So, goodbye for now. Or forever. I'm not sure. But what I do know is that it's time for me to live my legacy, not write it.

Sincerely,
Olive Lorusso

My Very Own Journey

By Adysen Glover

Alice was a nice girl. She had a few problems, but she knew how to handle them. She was fifteen, and all she could think about was turning eighteen so she could get away from the terrible town where she lived. She had a hard time communicating with others – especially guys. She had only ever had one boyfriend, and that was in seventh grade, so it didn't count because they were so young. Every time someone tried to talk to her, or be friends with her, she didn't know how to feel.

She thought maybe she couldn't connect with anyone because she had a hard life at home. It affected her everywhere she went. When she was only eight years old, her dad walked out on her. Although she thought she would get over this eventually, it troubled her a great deal. She was fifteen and still had a hard time when she saw a father with a little girl. She felt empty. She couldn't understand how it was to actually feel anything. That is what bothered her. When her dad left, her mom was really upset, but Alice never dealt with her feelings.

She was a freshman in high school, and it was not easy trying to keep up with everyone. She was on the basketball team, but she never talked to anyone on the team unless it was on the court. That made things hard for her because she was never at any of the other functions with the team – not because she didn't want to be, but because she was never invited. She knew about the big Christmas party because they had it every year. The only problem was that she knew she wouldn't be invited.

By Thanksgiving Break, the basketball team hadn't practiced in a while because they had a short season. They only made it to the first championship game but lost because they were all having an off-night. Their coach, Mark, was super mad and threatened to kick everyone off the team, even the ones who didn't play much. That was a rough ride home for everyone. After a few weeks, Mark forgave them, but he told them they were going to take a short break. They all knew that even though he had forgiven them, they would be required to begin every kind of workout he could possibly think of.

The team was starting practices again tomorrow, just two weeks before Christmas. This only gave Alice more to worry about. She knew right around the corner was the huge Christmas party, so she tried to think of every way to get people to like her. She tried talking to the other girls, but most of them just talked about guys or their boyfriends. She couldn't fit in with them because the only thing she ever felt was stress. That somehow made her feel more alive. She never appeared to be stressed, but on the inside, she was a mess. Sometimes, when she was at lunch, she would just sit in an older friend's car and stress so badly that she would shake. It had been a while since she had felt this stressed. Life had been pretty easy for her the past couple of weeks. All she had to focus on was school, so she didn't have to worry about basketball. She knew practice started again tomorrow, though. The more she thought about it, the more she found that she just did not care as much.

She was starting to think nothing she felt was real. Not even the stress. She had been contemplating quitting basketball even though she was really good. She just didn't see the point in

45

playing basketball anymore. Honestly, she didn't see the point in anything at all. Getting up for school every day had become a challenge because she didn't have any motivation. She got to the point where even getting up to go to the kitchen felt like a chore. Slowly, she introduced the idea of quitting the basketball team to her mom.

At first, her mom was hesitant about it because she knew just how much time and effort Alice had devoted to the sport. She told her if she still felt this way after two weeks, she could quit, but she would need to find something to be a part of. After the two weeks had passed, she, of course, still felt the same way. She knew she was done with basketball. She knew she was done with everything. She quit the team, and then she wanted to be homeschooled.

Her mom thought it would be best if she just stayed in school, partially because she wanted her to be focused on her work and not get distracted, but also because she knew she needed that social interaction. Alice was upset about not getting homeschooled, but she knew her mom was trying to do what was best for her because she knew she just wanted to see her succeed. After she quit basketball, her grades were better than ever, and she was the smartest kid in her grade. Even though she was only a freshman, she was already in classes with some of the juniors, and sometimes, she would even show them up.

In one of her classes that she had with some of the juniors, there were a lot of girls and only three guys, which was odd. The guy she knew was Andrew, from basketball. The boys had always practiced after the girls, and sometimes, they would scrimmage each other, so she remembered him because he was the best shooter on the team. Other than that, she knew a second guy's name was Ryan, and the only reason she knew that was because he was always getting into trouble. She didn't know the third guy. He always sat in the back of the classroom with his headphones on and his music playing full blast.

He always gave Alice a certain look with a little smirk. She thought he was cute, but she just assumed he was messing with her. Of course, she didn't really care because she never thought much about guys. Until the other day when she was late to class... She walked in as everyone else was about to start an assignment, and the teacher made her stand in front of the class and explain why she was late. For the first time ever, she felt embarrassed. She looked back at the last row of desks and saw the boy whose name she didn't know. He was already giving her that certain look, smirking at her like he always did, then continued what he was doing. Confused and still embarrassed, Alice started to feel that she was blushing.

She had never felt like this before, and she didn't know how to deal with it. That night, while she was lying in bed, she began to think about her dad and felt sad. She actually started feeling everything at once and started caring almost too much. All night long, she sat in bed, thinking and remembering. Every little thing that had ever hurt her feelings stirred her emotions, even the things that had made her happy. Her emotions were everywhere. She played sick the next day because she needed time to cope with everything she was feeling.

Two weeks later, she still wasn't going to school because, after a few nights, her mom had found her crying in her room. She thought it would be a good idea for her to see the doctor. This wasn't a normal doctor visit, like when she would get tested to see if she had the flu or something. This doctor visit was to determine if she would be diagnosed with depression, and if she could then get some medication to help. The diagnosis was positive, and the medicine was prescribed. The doctor told her she couldn't go to school for two weeks, for she would have to take her prescription every day. It didn't make her completely okay, but the only healing that it left was what she would have to do herself.

On the day before she went back to school, she received a text message: *Hey, it's Jake!*

She responded, *Hey, but I don't know you.*

As he continued to text her, he explained that he was the guy from class, the one who sat in the back row. They had English together. All they ever did was write or do little assignments. She figured he was texting her because he needed help with some of the work. After all, everyone knew she was the smartest girl in her grade.

That wasn't the case, though, because after a while, Alice finally asked why he had texted her. He told her that he thought she was wanting homeschooling, and he wanted to talk. She told him about her issues, and he begged for more information. He wanted to know what kind of issues she was having, and she told him.

He responded, *Yeah, in seventh grade I had to do that too, but I'm sorta better now.*

Sorta? she replied.

It took him hours to respond. Finally, he said, *Sorry, I was taking a nap. I've just been feeling kinda down lately.*

Then, Alice put it together. She knew what he had meant by 'sorta.'.

She went to school the next day and decided not to overthink things with Jake. When she went to English class, Jake looked at her, but it was different this time. This time, he looked at her in a reassuring way, a way that made her feel safe for the first time in two weeks.

She sat next to him in that class because she felt that she had connected with him. She'd never connected with anyone before, so this was new to her. A few minutes after she had sat down, Andrew and Ryan came over. Andrew usually sat with Jake, but since she was there, he was about to sit somewhere else. However, he decided he wanted her seat and asked for it. Jake grew defensive, so he said in a very aggressive tone, "She is fine sitting right there. You can sit in front of me."

Andrew didn't like the way Jake had spoken to him, but instead of saying anything, he decided just to leave it alone. Once everyone had settled in and started working on their writing assignment, Andrew turned around and asked her, "Why'd you quit the basketball team—you were really good?"

She just looked at him for a second, trying to think of the best thing to say. She ended up responding, "I just didn't enjoy playing anymore, and I knew I needed a break." He understood. Basketball took a lot of time and energy, and left little opportunity for anything else. They all started to talk and eventually arrived at the subject of school. Ryan said he was really smart, and was an A-and-B-role student. Jake was smart, but he just didn't like to show it. All Alice said was she had all A's. Ryan called her a nerd. This made Jake angry. He flipped over his desk onto Ryan. Then, he screamed at him and said never to say anything like that about Alice again.

The next day, Ryan didn't talk to Jake at all. That day, Jake caught up with Alice before lunch and asked if she wanted to eat lunch with him at one of the restaurants nearby. She said yes, because she kind of liked him. Yesterday, after school, from the time she got home until the time she went to bed, she stayed on the phone with him. They ate at the local burger restaurant. It was the hot spot for teenagers, and pretty much everyone in town. Alice and Jake talked for a while about childhood and life, in general. The next day, when they went back to school, they continued talking, all day long. However, when Alice got home that day, things went very wrong. She saw her mom lying on the kitchen floor passed out and bleeding. Immediately, she dialed 9-1-1. She waited about five minutes for the ambulance to arrive, and the police showed up. When the paramedics arrived, they pushed Alice aside so she couldn't see anything. She rode with them to the hospital, and the whole way there she was barely making it. When they reached the hospital, Alice's mom was taken straight into surgery.

The surgeons came out thirty minutes later and told her that her mom hadn't made it through the surgery because her head injury had been too significant. Alice was lost and didn't know what to do because her dad wasn't around and she didn't have anyone else to take care of her. She stayed at her house alone for three days, and didn't text, call, or speak to anyone. She decided she should go to school because that's what her mom would have wanted her to do. That morning, as she was getting ready, she heard a knock on the door. She opened it and saw three people standing outside. Two men and one woman. The men said they needed to look around for a minute, and the woman asked if there was a place where she and Alice could talk. Alice just walked, and the woman followed her. She proceeded to ask, "So, since your mom has unfortunately passed, you're going to need to stay with your legal guardian."

Alice told her that her dad hadn't been around since she was very young. The woman informed her that he was her legal guardian and that his name was Matthew Bradford. She said the police didn't have his address on file but promised to find him to determine if he was capable of keeping Alice for the next three years. The men and woman left. They said they would be back by the end of the day. When Alice checked her phone, she saw fifty messages from Jake.

She texted him and apologized for not texting him for the past couple of days. She promised to explain everything at school. He immediately texted back and said it was okay. She met him the next day in the parking lot before school, and they talked until they had to go to their first class. She told him she would finish explaining what had happened later. When they met in the parking lot again during lunch, she told him what had happened to her mom. She told him she didn't have anywhere to stay. She became emotional, and Jake comforted her, reassuring her that he would help her every step of the way. He told her if she needed a place to stay, she would be more than welcome to come stay with him, but he would have to talk to his parents first. It wouldn't be that big of a deal because he had his own place at his parents' house. It was not very big because it was meant to be a shed. She thought that would work, if all else failed with her dad. They went back to class. Before English, though, she ran to the bathroom. She felt sick. Jake saw her and rushed after her. He reached the bathroom as the bell rang. However, being late to class was the least of his worries. His biggest concern was Alice. Was she okay? She saw him as he came in with a worried look on his face. Suddenly, she realized that even though her dad had left, even though she had just lost her mom, someone still loved her.

He sat with her, and snuck her out of school, and then, they went to her house. He talked to her and helped her think of some different ways to get help. After that, they decided to rest their minds by watching a movie. They heard a knock on the door around 6 o'clock. It was the woman who said she was going to help her find her dad. She said she had found an address, and she and Alice would go meet with him tomorrow. Jake said he would go with them to support Alice.

They went and found out her dad was not a good person. The reason he wasn't around wasn't because he just wanted to leave. It was because her mom knew what was best, so she had kept Alice away from him. The truth was he was an addict and couldn't get clean for her mom or her. He explained the whole story and said he knew he had messed up but just couldn't stop. Alice started to cry when she heard the explanation. He began using drugs when he was a kid. He said life was hard when he was little because he had grown up in a bad environment. When he got older, he didn't know how to cope, so he started making bad decisions, leading to bad habits. When he met Alice's mom, he stayed clean for two years. The only problem was he couldn't continue anymore because he was tempted to start over again every day. One day, when her mom got home, she found him doing all the things she hated, so she told him to leave. So, he left and never looked back because he knew it was best for everyone. Alice started to argue and get upset because she thought life would have been ten times better if she had had some type of father figure around.

Jake had to pull Alice out of the house to get her to leave. He knew that the man who didn't deserve to be called her dad didn't care about her. He drove her back to her house and promised to stay with her through the night. "I don't want to be anywhere but with you tonight," he said.

She cried from the time they got home till early the next morning. Jake stayed up with her all night and told her it wasn't her fault that her dad had made bad decisions. Finally, she fell asleep, and he went to get clothes from his house. He came right back and fell asleep at her house. She woke up feeling stressed and down in the dumps. Jake told her that they were going to try to find someone to talk to because, although he could listen, he was no therapist. They met with various people trying to figure out who would be the best fit for her. She ended up deciding on

51

an older woman in her forties. She was going to have to meet with her every other day.

Slowly, she started seeing progress in her mental health. Jake started taking her to the gym, and she was starting to get in really good shape. A few months later, there was a knock on the door, and it was the police. Alice stepped outside to hear what they had to say. Apparently, what had happened to her mom wasn't an accident. Someone had pushed her. They had got a few fingerprints that night from the counter. They were her dad's. He was already in custody, and his court day was in a week.

She refused to let this bring her down, so she didn't go to court to see the results. The day that she was supposed to go she went out with Jake. She wanted him to know that she was no longer affected by her dad or his actions. Soon, she received a random phone call a couple of weeks later. It was from the jail. Her dad had been in an accident. There had been a huge fight. Another inmate had hit him with a plate. It had knocked him out and caused a brain bleed. They were treating him at the jail because he was not able to leave. There was only a small chance of him surviving. She thought of going because, after all, it was her dad. Finally, she got a call saying her dad wouldn't be able to hold out much longer. She went, even though she didn't really want to. She was two minutes too late. He was already gone. In a way she felt relieved, for the first time since her mom had passed. It finally seemed that it was over for her. Now, she and Jake could get married and live happily together for the rest of their lives.

Therapy

By Madison Hansen

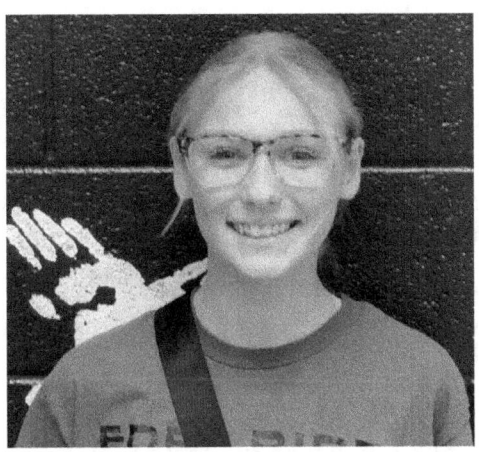

All I could see and hear were the lights and sirens of what seemed like hundreds of police cars and ambulances. I was crying so much that I could barely breathe. As the police officer loaded my husband into the patrol car, he started yelling at me, "ALICIA, I'M SORRY! I DIDN'T MEAN TO FALL ASLEEP AND ROLL OVER ON HUDSON!"

At this point, all of our neighbors were outside, sitting on their front porch swings, trying to look as if they were watching the sunset beyond their houses. Some were trying to look like they were sweeping. They looked at us curiously because they thought Parker and I were the perfect married couple. Of course, we had only been married for a few months before he killed our four-week-old baby by smothering him. Only five minutes after all the police cars and the ambulance left, I had at least fifty voicemails asking about the commotion. Once I sorted through the messages, I called one person back: my mom.

My mom and I had always been close, especially since she was a single mother who worked two jobs just to put me through school. My dad left when I was around a month old. Apparently, he ran off with a twenty-year-old woman and moved to Florida.

My mom and I talked almost every day for months after the tragedy. We talked about how our days were, and how I was coping. Today when she called, she brought up the new therapy facility.

"Therapy would be another amazing thing to help you," she said.

I began considering the idea of therapy when I started hearing the faint noises of a baby crying in Hudson's light blue room with clouds painted on the walls. Most nights, I went into the room, played with the toys he had barely gotten to play with, and sat in the rocking chair and cried. I texted my mom and told her I was going to start going to the therapy facility called *Mental Wellbeing*.

I was putting on a t-shirt and a pair of skinny jeans when the phone started ringing. I picked it up and heard a recording saying, "This is the Lincoln County Jail. Would you like to accept your husband's call?" His voice was the last voice I'd wanted to hear.

"Hey, Alicia, I just wanted to say I'm sorry. You know I didn't mean to roll over on Hudson," he said.

"I know you didn't mean to, but I still miss him. Do you know when you have to go to court?" I tried not to sound tired, like I had given up on life and had cried just ten minutes earlier in the bedroom we used to share.

"Tomorrow at 9 a.m. And try to dress nicely, please."

He still remembered how much I hated wearing dresses and skirts.

"Whatever," I said, annoyed.

"I'll see you tomorrow, I guess. I love you, Alicia."

Without saying *I love you too* like I used to, I hung up the phone. I went into our old room, grabbed some twenty-dollar bills from his top drawer, stuffed them into my purse, climbed into my car, and went to therapy.

The big sign with white LEDs around it said *Mental Wellbeing*. I pulled myself out of my car and started for the door. After just a few steps, though, I turned around and went back to my car. I could hear my mother's disapproving voice, so I froze in the middle of the parking lot. A few seconds later, a beautiful woman, around 5'3" approached me.

"Hey, I'm Bella. Do you need help? I work in that building, and I saw you pacing back and forth."

No wonder she looks perfect, I thought. *Even her name means beauty.*

"I'm sorry. My name's Alicia. I was going to go inside, but I'm having second thoughts," I said as I fought back tears. She started walking to the building, and I followed closely behind.

"Come on, I'll walk you to the waiting room."

The sound of absolute silence in the waiting room somehow relaxed and annoyed me at the same time. I began to bounce my leg as that was the only thing I could think of to keep myself calm. All of a sudden, the door was flung open, and Bella appeared in the doorway.

"Alicia!" she called loudly for the entire room, halfway full of people, to hear.

I stood and walked quickly to her.

"Follow me," she said as quietly as a whisper. "I'm going to be your therapist."

I did as I was told, and we walked into a room that had a desk, a couch, and a few chairs.

"You can move stuff around if you need to," she said. "Just make yourself at home."

I sat on the couch that had already been pulled up to her desk, and she handed me a form with questions like when was my birthday, what was my favorite color, what did I do for a living, and if I had any kids. As soon as I read this question, I started crying.

She came over to me and said, "What's wrong?"

"My husband accidentally suffocated my son and got put in jail," I said, struggling to get the words out.

Bella waited for me to stop crying before she asked any more questions, and I told her I wanted to go home. She led me out the door and walked me to my car. I texted my mom before I left the parking lot and told her I was leaving my therapy session. She said she was proud of me for going to therapy.

***

A Year Later

A year ago today was when Hudson died. I've visited his grave during every major holiday, and sometimes left a balloon or flowers. I still miss him very much, but I've gotten better. Parker still has four years left of jail. I've been going there to talk to him, but there is a pane of glass between us that's so thick, I have to use a phone to communicate. Yesterday while I was in a therapy session, Bella had an idea that made me curious. She was talking about how she had a patient a few years back who had gone through the same thing I did and ended up adopting a child.

I told my mother about the idea, and she said to tell Parker when I went to visit him. I read online that in order to adopt a child, it wasn't a good idea to have a husband who's in jail. I thought about a divorce because the apartment and car were in my name, so I wouldn't have to be homeless and could take the child to and from school.

I decided to go to the courthouse, get divorce papers, and drop them off at the jail. Around ten minutes later, my phone rang. I heard the same voice I heard every time he called me.

"This is the Lincoln County jail. Would you like to accept your husband's call?"

"Yes," I replied.

"I don't know what's wrong with you, but we are not getting a divorce," Parker said. I could feel his anger through the phone.

"We are getting a divorce. I want to adopt a child, and the orphanage won't let me do that with a husband in jail for murder!" I yelled and hung up.

I went by the jail the next day to see if he had signed the papers. The security guard came to me with papers in his hands and told me to file a restraining order against him before he got out of jail.

"I've seen something like this before, and the wife got murdered after." His deep voice added to my fear. I ran out without saying anything.

When I returned the divorce papers to the courthouse, I filled out the paperwork to file a restraining order.

"It takes around four months for the divorce to be finalized," said Judge Johnson, looking through the papers.

I went down to the orphanage like Bella had told me to do and saw the happiest little boy running around. His name was Kaden Lee Jackson, and he was four years old. I sat down on a couch and watched how nice and kind he was to all of his friends. He grabbed a toy car and sat beside me on the couch.

I looked at the director and whispered, "I want to adopt him." She brought the adoption papers, but she said the adoption process took a few months.

I spent the rest of the day in Walmart getting clothes, shoes, toys, and a car seat for him. I could barely sleep that night since I was so excited to adopt Kaden. As soon as I woke up every morning, I got ready and went to the orphanage to see him and filled out more and more of the numerous pages of paperwork.

I continued to see him for a few months until the day of my divorce with Parker was finalized. That day, I went to see Parker for the last time.

"I'm happy you have been trying to adopt a child after what happened to Hudson. I always knew you would be an amazing mother."

His words made me rethink everything I had done since Hudson's death. *No!* I thought. *I'm not going to be vulnerable again!*

"If you ever want to try again..."

"NO!" I yelled, interrupting his sentence.

"Okay, okay, sorry for asking, I guess."

"I guess? Really! You better be joking right now. You are a selfish, lying, rude person. You know what I'm happy about? I'm happy I divorced you!" I yelled and left.

I got into my car and raced to the orphanage. Kaden was the only person I could smile at after being mad at Parker. Kaden's smile somehow made me forget all of the bad things that had ever happened to me. My divorce. Hudson's death. My dad leaving. All of it.

I arrived at the orphanage to see the director with a wide smile.

"Today's the day!" she said excitedly.

"What do you mean 'todays'?"

"Today's the day you can bring Kaden home!"

I ran inside to see him, and he was waiting with a bigger smile than the director's. He had a backpack on that was almost as big as he was. He ran to me and gave me a hug. After he said goodbye to all of his friends, we went to my car and drove home.

After a couple of months, I started hanging out with friends, and their kids met my son. Finally, I'm so thankful for my mom. Without her, I wouldn't have gone to therapy; therefore, I wouldn't have Kaden.

Unexpected

By Sydney Lawrence and Caelyn Gilliard

I grabbed my coffee and went to my seat. It was around six o'clock in the morning, and I did not want to be at work. The police station soon filled up with policemen who were already in a bad mood. A fairly large car accident had happened earlier, and people had to go to work early.

"Lydia," Chief Matthew said, sounding annoyed, "there is a meeting in the conference room. Finish whatever you're doing and meet the rest of the forensics team and me there." I looked at him and glanced across the room. I could see into the conference room from where I was sitting. The projector was set up, and there were two or three other people in there, waiting for the meeting to start.

"Yes, sir, I will be there as soon as possible," I muttered. I put the papers I was filling out into a drawer and walked to the conference room.

The cold room soon filled with other people, and Chief Matthew stood up. "Alright, everyone, settle down!" he shouted. I did not want to be here. "We have a very important case we need to discuss. I am sure most of you already know about the unidentified murderer who has killed a young girl." He paused and looked around the room. "Lydia, could you please come up here and tell us about the case?"

"Yes, sir." I walked towards the front of the room and started speaking. "My job is to analyze crime scenes and collect evidence. Currently, we have zero suspects. The only thing we know is that the victim is Annebeth Jones, and she was killed in an abandoned trailer park." I rolled my eyes. There were only three people who didn't look totally miserable.

"Thank you, Lydia," Chief Matthew said as he collected the papers on the podium in front of him. "Everyone, return to whatever you were doing. Meeting dismissed." He walked out of the conference room, and several followed. The meeting lasted barely five minutes, but it was still important. Sorta.

I sat down at my desk and laid out the 'evidence' I was writing down in my journal. It wasn't true evidence. It was only things I had noticed when I went to the scene.

Journal: Evidence #1
9/15/1980

The trailer park was already sketchy. It was abandoned, dirty, rusty, and in the middle of nowhere. I assumed Annebeth wasn't alone in an odd place like that. She was probably exploring with some of her friends. I'll be going to the local newspaper station to warn others to be cautious. There were around seven different trailers in the area. The red trailer was clean, probably the cleanest one in the trailer park. It was a tiny one-bedroom and one-bathroom trailer. No furniture, either. The bathroom was the only room that didn't have white walls. Instead, they were blood red. It was where she was killed, but it was odd the murderer did not clean the only room that could have been used as evidence. It is like he is giving us clues...kinda like a sign. A sign more blood will be spilled.

The newspaper station was a ten-minute walk from my office. When I got to the front lobby, the woman at the front desk said that Bethany, the newspaper reporter, never showed up, and that she never called to say that she was sick or anything.

"May I go to her office and look around?" I asked, trying not to sound like a creep.

"Go on. Please tell me if you find anything," the lady said. "Her office is up the stairs and to the left." She put her cigarette in her mouth and shooed me away. I nodded and went up the stairs, down the long hallway, and to the newspaper woman's office.

I slowly entered her office. It was a large and fancy room. It had a big sofa underneath the window seal with large pots of orchids on each end table. Her desk area had scattered newspapers and a bottle of ink that had spilled on top of them. I walked to the desk and pressed my finger in the black ink. "Still wet," I said to myself as I jogged towards the exit of the room.

"Sorry, ma'am, I did not see anything, but I have one question. Is Bethany messy? Is her room usually clean or chaotic?" I asked the lady at the front desk, who was still holding a cigarette.

"The times I have been in there, it has been very nice. Her papers were in nice stacks, and everything was in her filing cabinet," she responded.

"Thank you, have a nice day," I said while walking outside. I grabbed the letter Bethany had written me a few days ago out of my pocket.

9/13/1980

Dear Lydia,

I'm Bethany from the newspaper office, and I recently found out about the murder. I would be happy to put anything in the next local paper about it if you would like. I have also done some research on it, and I may have a lead. My address is written below, so you can stop by and we can look at the evidence. If one of my suspects is the murderer, then we need to arrest him. I know you

*work in forensics, so hopefully, all my evidence
adds up. 1238 Iris Circle is my address. Thank you.*
  Best of luck,
  Bethany Hart

I had decided that I was going to research Annebeth Jones, but someone else had claimed that duty. Instead, I was taking it upon myself to warn the town about the killer since Chief Matthew had decided not to do anything or tell anyone. When I walked inside, I ran into Leo, our newest cop, and got an idea. I grabbed him by the wrist and pulled him outside.

"Woah, Lyd—what's going on?" he said.

"We're going to Bethany Hart's house," I replied. "I think she is in danger." I continued dragging him out the door.

"Who's that?" Leo asked.

"I'll explain in the car! Just...get...in!!" I replied as I struggled to drag him to my pickup truck.

"Sounds like fun," he said with sarcasm thick in his voice.

I rolled my eyes. "So much fun." He gritted his teeth, and of course, so did I. I hated him sometimes, but he meant well.

Leo started the car, and I told him where to turn. I am familiar with Iris Circle because my adoptive parents used to live here. "Bethany's office was messy, and there was a bottle of spilled ink that was still wet," I told Leo.

"That's odd," he replied. "I thought the woman at the front desk said she wasn't there at all today, right?"

"Right," I said. When we got there, her car was in the driveway, so we walked up the steps and knocked. One minute...two minutes...three minutes. There was still no answer.

Leo opened the door and looked at me, giving me a grin. "It's unlocked," he said, and I responded with a questioning look. I mean, how can a cop willingly break into someone's house? We walked in and glanced around the living room and kitchen.

"You check upstairs, and I'll check down here," I said, as Leo walked up the stairs and started looking around. The dishes were left in the sink, and there were papers everywhere. "Bethany!?

Where are you?" I called out, desperately looking everywhere I could.

I heard Leo scream, and my heart stopped beating. I grabbed a kitchen knife and ran upstairs, ready for anything. I saw him staring wide-eyed at the lifeless body of Bethany Hart.

Her blood had spilled across her bedroom, which had a similar layout to her office. The oddest thing was there was a bottle of ink that had spilled onto multiple papers, just like it was in her office. Leo grabbed his walkie talkie and said, "Dispatch! I need you immediately!"

"Where are you?" a cop replied in a static voice.

"1238 Iris circle," I said.

"On the way with two others."

"What do we do from here?" Leo asked me.

"I don't know," I replied. I truly did not know. The feeling I felt was like a void, just–nothing. I touched the spilled ink, and it was still wet. Just like in her office. Then, I realized something. "Leo, the killer might still be here."

"I am already stressed about this–are you trying to break me?" he snapped as he slammed his fist on the nearest table.

I winced. "I'm sorry, I forgot," he said, clearly noticing my reaction. My parents had fought a lot, so I always got upset when someone did that.

"It's okay, but we still need to look around," I replied. Then, we heard sirens and ran downstairs to meet the officers who had been sent. Leo went and met them. I couldn't hear what he was saying from the porch, but one officer talked into his walkie talkie. Probably calling for an ambulance.

Journal: Evidence #2
9/17/1980
I was right. Of course I was. It was pretty much expected that this killer was not finished. Although I knew he or she was coming back for more, I guess I just didn't expect it to be Bethany. After the ambulance had carried out her dead body, I found some of the letters she was going to send through

> *the mail. They were written about who she thought might be the murderer. The names were Aimee Bowman and Aarin Brock. I will be doing more research and background checks on the two, and I'll question them, if possible. Even if I did not get to meet Bethany, I do believe she was trying to help us. Most of the evidence was lost due to the ink spill, but I still took the letters with me. I tested for DNA while the ink was still wet, but only Bethany's DNA came up on the spill. Whoever this is knows what they're doing.*

Leo and I were doing background checks for the three suspects. "So, Aimee Bowman, hmm...," he said.

"Anything on her record?" I turned to look at the paper I had written the names on to make sure I had spelled the suspect's name correctly. "I'm not seeing anything for her, except for vandalism a few years ago," I said.

"Vandalism is so scary," Leo said with sarcasm.

"We still need to interrogate her," I replied.

"What about the other suspect?" Leo asked.

I responded, "His records are clean, as far as I can see."

Leo turned to look at me. "Does that mean we don't have to do an interrogation on him?" He spoke almost as if he were pleading.

I turned around, put my hands on my hips, and said, "What kind of question is that? We still need to. Many people's lives could depend on it."

"Dang it," he responded, to which I rolled my eyes. I had the sudden urge to slap him.

"Just because the other suspect's records are clean doesn't mean she didn't kill the victims; in fact, it could mean that she is more likely to be the murderer," I said.

"Yeah, yeah," he responded.

I threw the closest object I could find, which happened to be a paper cup, at him.

"Ouch," he said while rolling his eyes as if doing an impression of me. He threw the cup back at me, and I caught it. He put his hands on his hips, rolled his eyes, and said "Ooh, I know how to catch things!" in a horrible impression of my voice. I walked out of the room, and he ran up to me and dragged me back into the room.

"Why am I not allowed to leave?" I asked him.

"I was recreating you dragging me to the truck," he exclaimed. I couldn't deal with him any longer, so I decided to go home to lunch and act like I was leaving for the day. "Bye, Leo!" I yelled as I was walking out the door.

The car ride home was fairly quick. I live in a small apartment complex five miles from the police station. The drive was peaceful, and I got home earlier than I usually do. I fixed myself a ham sandwich on my small countertop. I decided to go to my room to read a book. About two hours later, having forgotten I should be at work, I heard a knock on my front door. When I opened the door, I saw Leo awkwardly standing there. He said, "There was another murder. Chief asked me to come get you."

"Who?" I asked as I frantically put my black combat boots on.

"Charlotte Collier, that's her name. We know nothing else about her," he said.

"Isn't she the cashier at the local market?" I asked.

"Yes, she was," he said. "Now, come on. We need to hurry."

"Okay," I said as I followed him to his car.

"Well, I have no clue what to do when we get there," Leo said.

"Did they tell you to do anything?" I asked. "I'll obviously be looking for evidence."

"They didn't tell me anything but her name and to get you," he replied.

I was tying my boots in his front seat. "Well, that's useful," I said. He was looking at me funny and seemed really uncomfortable about something.

"What's wrong?" I asked him.

"Just, all of these murders are getting to me. It seems like me, you, and the families of the victims don't get a second to relax," Leo murmured.

"It'll be okay," I said, trying to reassure him.

By then we had reached the police station. I was running towards the evidence room. Dr. Crystal Briggs was already there. "Hello, Lydia," she said. I put on my lab coat and gloves and came over. "I think we need to start with DNA testing," she said.

"Okay," I replied.

Charlotte had charming blonde hair and light skin. She was beautiful and so nice at the market. I don't know how anyone could kill someone that kind—or anyone, to be honest. She had one large stab wound right through the heart. "Dr. Morgan, should we do an autopsy?" she asked as I carefully examined the injury.

"Yes, we need to check out the internal damage," I responded. The autopsy lasted only forty-five minutes. The stab had reached the heart, though. Leo and I left soon after because he didn't have anything to do. When we got home, I started throwing some grilled cheese and soup together for us.

"What were the results of the autopsy?" he asked once we had sat down.

"She had one stab wound that reached her heart," I said. "There was nothing else."

"Were there even signs she had fought them off?" he asked.

"I think she just accepted her fate and let him kill her. Or she was asleep," I said.

"I hope she was asleep," Leo responded.

"Me, too," I murmured.

"You sound like something's wrong...," he said with a questioning look.

"Oh—um...everything's fine," I said.

He raised his eyebrow, and I couldn't help but laugh. Leo reached over and tousled my dark brown hair. I put my hand against my chest and said, "How dare you," in a sarcastic tone.

He just rolled his eyes, saying, "I'm going to bed, goodnight."

"Night," I responded. I decided to go to bed too. It had been a long day.

***

A few days later, I was still trying to figure out who the murderer was. None of the clues were adding up. The only thing that seemed to make sense was that only females had been killed, and only weapons had been used. No poison. Annebeth Jones had been killed in a bathtub with multiple stab wounds in the arms, legs, and throat. Bethany Hart had been killed with a gunshot wound to the head, and Charlotte had one clear cut through the heart. The three victims had suffered, but there were many differences among the cases that did not make sense.

I tied my boots and put my jacket on. After I walked out the door and down the steps of my apartment complex, I grabbed my mail out of my mailbox and walked to my car. There was one letter from my mother. It was in a teal envelope. When I opened it, I saw the words "Happy Birthday!" with a five-dollar bill inside. It was thoughtful of my mom to get me a birthday card, but I was surprised it had arrived the day of my birthday. Had she sent it early so it would arrive today? I didn't know.

"Leo?" I said, walking into the police station. A few days had passed since the last victim was murdered.

"Yes?" he said as he stood up.

"I'm going to go look for evidence around town. Would you like to come?"

"Now, why would I want to do that?" he said in a sarcastic tone.

"Because I asked you to," I said, rolling my eyes.

"Okay," Leo sighed. "You know where it's at?"

He stood up and walked toward me.

"No, not yet. I will go and ask Chief Matthew." I walked to the chief's office and knocked on the door. "Hello? Chief Matthew?" I patiently waited for what seemed like an eternity for him to open the door.

I could faintly hear him mumble something under his breath, but I could not make out what he was saying. Chief Matthew opened the door just enough to peek out. "What do you want, Lydia? I'm busy," he groaned. Chief could tell I was going to ask something he did not want to deal with.

"I was going to ask if Officer Leo and I could go to the most recent murder scene? I would like to gather some evidence because I didn't get the chance earlier." I tried to ask in a way that wouldn't make him angrier, but I guess I failed. Annoyed, he sent me off to my desk and told me my work was irrelevant.

"Sorry, Leo, we're out of luck. Chief said no," I muttered as I dragged my feet to my messy desk.

"Do we have to listen to him, though?" Leo asked.

"We don't have to, but it's still not right," I responded.

"You should learn to break rules, especially if it is for the greater good," he said while tapping a pencil on the table and with his feet propped up on my desk. He had shuffled some of my papers to the edge so he could have more room.

I just rolled my eyes, "You were probably the biggest troublemaker in school."

"I was the teacher's pet, thank you very much!" he exclaimed.

"Whatever," I said in a sarcastic tone.

"So, what will it be, Lyd? Are we going, or not?" Leo whispered while he impatiently waited for me to answer.

"I don't know. Just give me a minute. There is some paperwork I need to finish." My journal and notebook paper were on the very edge of my desk, thanks to Leo. I grabbed my journal. I had not written much about the murders lately, but there hadn't been much to write. Chief Matthew was not even allowing me to leave the station, much less gather evidence. "I'll write another day," I told myself.

After ten minutes spent finishing some paperwork, I put everything away. My journal went into my purse so I could take it home, and the paperwork went back into the file. "Alright, Leo, let's go. I'll go on break, and you should, too." I grabbed my purse with my wallet inside and started towards the front door. Leo grabbed his bottle of water and a small box with a bow on it. He had a large grin on his face. He followed me to my car. "That's odd," I said. "Chief Matthew's car is gone."

"That is weird. I thought you said he had to do paperwork?" Leo said as he shut the car door and gave me the small box. "Here, open it." He nudged my hand, and I grabbed the box.

"Why are you giving this to me?" I asked.

"It's for your birthday. I didn't really know what you wanted," Leo murmured.

I opened the small box. There was a badge inside. "Thank you, Leo, but you do realize I have one of these, right?" I looked at him, and he pointed to the small writing engraved on the badge. It said "POLICE OFFICER" in large letters, unlike my badge that had "FORENSICS INVESTIGATOR" engraved on it.

"Now, you can be a part of the police force," he said, giving me a half smile.

"How did you even get an extra one?" I asked.

"You really don't know how to quit asking questions and just be grateful," Leo muttered. I put the badge in my pocket and started the car. The drive didn't last long, and when we arrived at the scene, there wasn't very much there. The murder had happened outside a gas station. I had not been told any details about when it happened, but I assumed it was late at night. Too bad there weren't any witnesses I could ask.

"Did they tell you where it happened?" I asked as I looked around the empty parking lot.

"It didn't happen over here. The victim's car was over here, and yes, there was blood in it, but her body was found over there in the woods," Leo said as he pointed at a large area of trees.

I got out of the car and started walking towards it. Leo followed behind me, and we approached the edge of the large pine trees. It was dark. If the sun weren't straight above us, we would need a flashlight. I went into the forest first, and he followed. "Do you remember where it happened?" I asked.

"It should be somewhere over...there. I see some caution tape that was never taken down." Leo pointed at some trees in the distance. Two of the trees had some neon yellow caution tape attached to them.

"I'll go first. Stay close behind me, Leo," I said. I was nervous to go by myself.

"Sorry, Lydia, I left my gun in the car. I'll be right back!" he said, jogging back to my car.

"Wait!–" I was hesitant to go on without him. Something was telling me not to go, but I went anyway.

There was a large tree stump near the area with the caution tape. It had a large axe in the center with dried blood on the blade.

I heard footsteps behind me. "Hey, Leo! I found something that might be useful." I turned around, and my heart stopped. A tall, dark figure was standing behind me with a knife in hand. The strange figure started charging towards me, and I froze. I didn't know what to do. "Run, run!" the voice in my head told me, but I just stood there.

Wait. My pocket. The badge, the badge! I pulled it out of my pocket and held it with the small pin sticking out. The killer was a few feet from me, so I tried to run to my right. The figure raised his knife, but luckily, he wasn't facing me yet. I raised the badge and jammed the pin into his hand. Thankfully, his gloves were thin. "Aghh!" he groaned as he dropped the knife and turned to face me.

"That voice sounds familiar," I told myself as I slowly backed up. The killer walked toward me and made a fist with each of his hands. "No...no...no!" the voice in my head shouted. I had backed into a tree. I couldn't risk going anywhere. "This has to be the murderer," I thought. I closed my eyes and hoped my passing would be painless. *Thump!* The figure's body hit the ground. I saw Leo standing behind him with his gun in hand. "Did you...?" I stared at the body.

"No...no. I knocked him out," Leo said.

"Okay," I responded.

Leo pulled me up. "You okay?" he asked.

"Yeah," I said. He didn't look convinced. He grabbed my arms and checked them. "I'm okay," I said in a stern voice.

"Okay, okay," he said as he dropped my arms. "Dispatch, I need you behind the gas station," he said.

"Ten-four," a policeman said. I walked over to the killer, lifted his hood, and gasped.

"What?" Leo said as he walked over. Then, he stared with wide eyes at the murderer.

The killer was Chief Matthew. "No wonder he didn't seem to care—he was the murderer this whole time," I said.

We saw the cops coming our way, and Leo explained what had happened. I still couldn't fathom it. What was his motive? How could he be so evil? So many questions were swimming in my head, all of them unanswered, but I guess I'll find out at the trial.

Journal: Final Evidence
12/4/1980
Matthew was put on trial a few days after he attempted to attack me. He was convicted of first-degree murder for planning everything out. He admitted that he had arranged all the murders, and that was why he was so busy with 'paperwork' all of the time. Sadly, the police could not get him to admit why he had murdered all those people. He got life in prison with no possibility of parole. Matthew hurt many families, and no one even knows why. He traumatized Leo and me. I was so stupid for not noticing it earlier. He was hateful and never let me help find evidence. No one else was aware that Matthew was killing all those people, but I think they're lying. This was all unexpected.

The Abandoned Hospital

By Kayannah McDonald and Ryleigh Hackert

Hi, my name is Anne Carter. I am thirteen and in eighth grade. Let me tell you a traumatizing story about me and my two best friends, Elias and Olivia.

***

Monday, October 19th. I was in school talking to Elias, my best friend since first grade.

"Hey, Elias, where is Olivia?" I asked.

"Olivia is in the classroom talking to the math teacher," replied Elias.

Walking to the math room, I passed a poster on the board in the hallway. It read, "Science competition on Wednesday." I ripped it down and ran back to Elias, showing him the poster.

"Elias! Look at this poster!" I yelled.

"Science competition? Since when do you like science?" said Elias.

"I have the best idea about what we can do! It says right here that we can explore any place in our city. We can go to the abandoned hospital down the road from my house!" I exclaimed.

"Is that really the best idea, though?" asked Elias.

Olivia, my and Elias's best friend, walked over to us. "Hi, guys, I'm back," she said.

"What did the math teacher have to say?" asked Elias.

"Oh, he was just talking about the grade I made on my test," Olivia replied.

"Was it a good grade?" Elias asked.

"I found this poster about a science competition!" I said before Olivia could answer Elias.

"Science competition?" Olivia said. "I didn't know you liked science, Anne?"

"That's what I said!" yelled Elias.

"I don't!" I exclaimed. "I just want to explore an abandoned hospital!"

"I don't know if that's a good idea," said Olivia.

"Blah, blah, blah," I mumbled.

"What if we get hurt?" said Elias.

"We won't, Scaredy Cat," I replied.

***

The next day came quickly. We did not want to get caught sneaking around the abandoned hospital, so we had to come up with a plan.

"What are we going to do about your parents?" Olivia said.

"Um, I will...tell them I am...going to your house!" I said.

"Ok...but what about my mom?" Olivia asked.

"Tell her you are going to come to my house!" I replied.

"Guys, what should I tell my dad?" asked Elias.

"That you are going to my house," said Olivia. None of our parents ever talked to each other, so we knew we would be fine.

I was so excited, I could not wait for tomorrow. That day, we went to class just like a normal day. The next day came slowly this time.

***

"Today is the day!" I thought when I woke up on Wednesday. I got to school and ran to Olivia.

"AH, OLIVIA, TODAY IS THE DAY WE GET TO GO TO THE HOSPITAL!" I yelled. A few people overheard me and gave me

73

nasty looks. "Did I say something wrong? Why is everyone giving me those looks?"

"Why do you think?" Olivia said. "You just said we are going to the hospital out loud!"

"Yeah? Well, we are," I responded.

"People are going to think we are actually going to the hospital for help! You forgot to say *abandoned*!" Olivia exclaimed.

"Oh, yeah...," I said.

"I don't think we should even say *abandoned* or *hospital*; people might think we're crazy," Elias continued while walking toward me and Olivia.

"Why are you guys not excited?" I asked Olivia and Elias.

"Maybe because we could get seriously hurt!" exclaimed Elias.

"Bingo!" said Olivia.

"Whatever!" I said. "I'm not gonna let party poopers ruin my fun."

"We are not trying to ruin your fun, Anne!" yelled Olivia while she was grabbing her hairbrush out of her locker.

"Fine! We will go if it means that much to you!" Elias said.

"Listen, I'm not making you guys go; I just think it will be fun," I said.

"It's fine, we will go," Olivia said while brushing her hair and putting away her hairbrush. Time passed slowly until 4:00 p.m.

***

"It is time to go!" I said while getting ready to go to the abandoned hospital.

"Ok, ok, we are coming," replied Elias.

"Do not forget the tent we are sleeping in tonight," Olivia said.

"Oh yeah, let me grab that," I responded. I went to my attic and started to pull down the ladder. Dust and spider webs fell out of the attic onto the floor. I climbed up the ladder and searched for the tent. I finally found it and grabbed it. I started to climb back down the ladder when, all of a sudden, I heard something. I couldn't see what it was, so I just ignored it. I climbed back down and shut the attic door.

***

"Alright, let's do this," Elias said. We started to walk down the driveway, which led to the road. We walked for a while until we finally reached the hospital.

"Alright guys, we are here," Olivia stated.

"WAIT! PLEASE DO NOT GO IN THERE!" I heard from behind me. I turned around and saw an old man with many scratches and bruises all over his face and legs. He looked like he had just fought a monster.

"What do you mean?" asked Olivia.

"THAT PLACE IS HAUNTED! I ALMOST DIED IN THERE! PLEASE DO NOT GO IN THERE!" the man begged.

"Whatever, he's probably just trying to prank us," I whispered. I told the old man that we were not going in there even though I was just trying to make him leave us alone. He walked away, so Olivia, Elias, and I went farther up the driveway.

"Oh look, here is a perfect place to set up our tent," suggested Elias. We set it up and put all of our gear inside.

"Alright, let's go in!" I exclaimed. I tried to knock on the door, but it opened by itself, or so I thought. A loud *CREEAAAK* is all we heard.

"Are you sure about this Anne?" asked Olivia.

"I'm really sure," I said to her.

"But what about the old man?" Elias replied.

"What about him?" I said.

"Well, he did say he went in there and almost died," Elias said in a worried voice.

"Yeah," Olivia chimed in.

"Like I told Olivia, he was just trying to scare us," I told Elias.

"Ok...," replied Elias.

"What are we even looking for?" Olivia asked.

"Yeah?" asked Elias.

"I don't really know," I replied. "I just wanted to come here for fun, you know?"

We walked in slowly and finally reached the lobby. Spider webs were everywhere.

"Eww, why is it so gross in here?" asked Olivia.

"Probably because it's old and abandoned," replied Elias.

"Guys, shut up and come on!" I exclaimed. We started to make our way towards the stairs.

"Guys...," Olivia stuttered. "I just stepped on something." I turned on the flashlight and pointed it towards her. "OH, MY GOODNESS!" she screamed while jumping. "IT'S A BODY BAG!" I could not believe my eyes. A body bag! Was there a real dead body in there?

"Oh my gosh, oh my gosh, oh my gosh!" I whispered. "How do we know if there's a body in there or not?"

"There obviously is!" Elias said while rolling his eyes.

"Elias, right now is not the time to be smart with me!" I said.

"It doesn't matter, we just need to get away from it!" Olivia yelled.

"Should we go up the stairs?" I asked Elias and Olivia.

"Sure, why not?" Elias responded.

"I do not care; I just want to get away from this thing," Olivia replied, seemingly unable to look away from her grisly discovery. We started up the stairs. I was in front, Olivia was in the middle, and Elias was in the back. As we went up the stairs, it got scarier and scarier.

"There are so many rooms!" Elias said.

"Let's try that one!" I said, pointing to an open room.

"No, I want to go to this one!" Olivia exclaimed while pointing to a closed room, maybe a patient room.

"Guys, how about we split up?" Elias asked.

"Ok!" I said, "that sounds good to me."

"Alright, I guess." Olivia answered.

"Meet back here in ten minutes," Elias said. We all walked away from each other and went to different rooms. I went to the open room which looked like a living room. There was a scratched-up couch and chair, and a TV with mold on it. Why was there mold? I was exploring the room when I heard a scream.

"HELP ME!" Elias screamed.

"Is that Elias?" I thought to myself. I ran toward the voice.

"Elias, are you alright?" I asked. No answer. "Elias?"

"Haha!" Elias said while laughing. "I got you guys!"

"Seriously, Elias!?" Olivia said while running to us.

"I hate you!" I said to Elias.

"Yeah, yeah," Elias said. "It was just a friendly joke."

"Nothing about that was funny!" exclaimed Olivia.

"Ok, I'm going back. Do not do that again, Elias," I said.

"Whatever...," replied Elias. I can't trust him. I went back to the living room, still confused about the mold on the TV. I found a door near the couch and chair. It was slightly hidden, so I was not sure if it led to an important room. I tried it, but it was locked. Where could the key be? I searched up and down until I found it. It was on the door frame. I unlocked the door and found more stairs. I had to tell the others.

"Elias!" I hollered. "Olivia!"

"What?" Olivia replied, walking over to me.

"Yes?" Elias said.

"I found a door in the room!"

"Let's explore it then!" Olivia said.

As we walked toward the door, Elias began talking. "Why are there more stairs?" he asked.

"Hospitals have many floors, Elias," Olivia replied.

"Ok, guys, are we going?" I asked.

"Yep, let's go!" Elias said.

We walked up the stairs that led to another door. This time it was not locked. We slowly entered and found a room full of cribs.

"Oh, it looks like a nursery!" said Olivia.

"Yeah!" replied Elias.

As we continued exploring, we found another door. It was slightly cracked open, and the lightbulb beyond was flickering. I heard crying and the sound of someone else trying to console it.

"What is that noise?" asked Elias.

"It sounds like a baby," replied Olivia.

"That can't be!" Elias said. "This hospital has been abandoned for years."

"Well, let's check it out," I replied.

Elias went in first, then me, then Olivia. "What is that noise now?" he asked.

"I do not know; it kind of sounds like a...." That's when a zombie popped out from behind the door.

"OH, MY GOSH!" Olivia yelled. "RUN!"

This time, Elias was in the back. He screamed. It was a real scream this time, like one out of a horror movie. I wanted to save him, but I was too scared to turn around. I heard Olivia trip and fall behind me.

"Olivia, get up fast!" I shouted.

"Keep running, Anna! I've hurt my leg!" Olivia yelled.

"No, come on, I didn't get to save Elias. I am going to save you!" We had just escaped the nursery when I realized I had scraped my knee on the door.

"Anna, my leg hurts so bad!" she cried.

We called a taxi and went to the hospital. The doctors said Olivia needed to stay in the hospital for a few days while they tried to figure out what was wrong with her leg.

What were we going to tell our parents? Elias was gone, Olivia had something wrong with her leg, and I only had a scrape on my knee. How are they going to believe me?

"Anna, this hurts bad," Olivia told me. "What is my mom going to say? What are we going to tell Elias's dad?"

"We will tell his dad the truth," I said. "We will tell your mom you tripped and fell in a huge ditch. I will tell my mom we were walking, and I tripped and fell trying to run from an aggressive dog. That's how I got the scape on my knee," I said.

"Ok...," Olivia replied.

***

Olivia's mom came into the hospital two days later. I went to the waiting room while her mom visited. Then, I heard a siren and a scream.

"Code blue! Code blue!" It was coming from Olivia's room. I wasn't able to see her, but I saw her leg; it was purple – dark purple.

"OLIVIA!" I screamed. A nurse saw me and told me that the doctors had to amputate her leg. What had I done? Elias was gone, Olivia lost her leg, and it was all my fault! How was I going to tell Elias's dad? He would never forgive me. I went home for the night but couldn't sleep. I stayed up thinking about all my memories of Elias. I finally drifted off. When I woke up, I decided to go to the hospital.

***

"Hello?" I peeked into Olivia's room after her surgery.

"Hi, Anna. I'm scared," Olivia said.

"It's ok," I told her. I saw that her leg was gone, and to be honest, I was terrified, too.

She was in the hospital for the next three days. I saw her once; then my mom said I couldn't go anymore. Olivia didn't go to school for the next two weeks. Then, I got the sad news on the phone.

It was Olivia. She told me she was leaving. Her parents were going to teach her at home.

I decided I would visit her every day, if she was up to it. We had fun. I told her all about what happened in school, and she told me what it was like having her parents for teachers. We did this for a long time.

A very long time. Oliva and I stayed friends forever. We are now in a nursing home together and someone had to hear the real story.

Murder at Camp

By Estrellita Trejo Medina and Kinsley Burton

"Alright, everybody, go back to your tents, and remember not to leave them until 6:00 A.M.!" my teacher, Mr. Johnson, said.

It was about 9:00 P.M. at the time, and we had just finished making smores at the campfire. We were all heading back to our tents to go to sleep. Then, around 11:00 P.M., I got the 'all clear' text from the group chat between my friends and me. I snuck out of my tent quietly and started walking into the woods, using my phone as a flashlight. As soon as I got to the creek, about a ten-minute walk from the campsite, I saw all my friends hanging around and talking. Well, almost all of them: My best friend Lydia was missing, so there were only Matthew, Jess, Nick, and Chase. I thought nothing of Lydia's not being there since she usually fell asleep early. Nick, my best guy friend, asked if anyone was up to explore the woods. Of course, being bored teenagers, we all said yes almost immediately. About fifteen minutes later, as we were walking down a bright path lit by the flashlights from everybody's phones, I started to smell something weird. It smelled kind of like metal. It was getting stronger with every step we took. I decided to say something about it because I was getting a bad feeling.

"Guys, do you smell that too, or am I going crazy?"

Matthew looked around and said, "Yeah, but I wouldn't worry about it; it's probably just a deer someone shot too close to the camp."

We all trusted him because he usually went hunting with his dad. I just nodded. A little while later, the smell grew worse, as if we were standing right next to where it was coming from. I had a really bad feeling by then and decided to go back to camp, but as I started walking away, I tripped over something. When I got up and dusted my knees off, I turned my flashlight around to see what I had fallen over. I froze. It was a dead body. I screamed so loudly, it echoed through the trees, and everyone came running toward me. The longer I looked, the more I thought the girl looked familiar. That's when I realized that the dead body I was staring at was Sarah. Sarah and I had been friends forever, and our moms were best friends, too. Sure, we weren't as close as we used to be, but we were still friends. Why would someone do something like that to her?

Someone shook me and started yelling at me to go back to camp. That's when I realized that a teacher had shown up and was trying not only to call the police but also to tell a group of hysterical teenagers to back up and go back to camp. By the time we had made it back, most of the teachers were awake and making us all sit down around the campfire to wait until the cops showed up. About thirty minutes later, they arrived.

"You have the right to remain silent; anything you say or do may be used against you in the court of law." The police put us in handcuffs, one by one, and put us in the back of the cop cars. I couldn't believe that this is happening. *Why do they think we did that? Why do they think we would ever do that to her?* We arrived at the police station around two hours later, and the police took our fingerprints and mugshots. They asked us what we were doing in the woods, and finally put us in a holding cell while they called our parents. I waited for my mom to come pick me up.

It was a seven-hour drive from town to the camp. Jessica and I were sharing a cell. She managed to fall asleep, but I couldn't. I stayed up until my mom arrived to pick me up. When Jessica and I were released from our cell, I ran up to Mom and gave her a huge hug. I was able to fall asleep in the car, but I woke up a little bit before we got home. Sarah's mom was there, and I couldn't look at her without crying. I walked up to her and gave her a hug. I couldn't imagine what she must have been going through, or even what she was thinking of. Her only child was dead. My friend was dead. I had to find out who did this, not only for me but for Sarah's mom, as well. A few hours later, my mom told me that the sheriff had given the town a curfew until the police found the killer. He was sure to give my group of friends and me a curfew until we were interrogated. The curfew was set for 8:00 P.M. on weekdays and 10:00 P.M. on weekends. They'd concluded the murder was premeditated, one for which the killer must have had a motive. I understood why they'd reached that conclusion because I'd seen the body. Someone killed my friend, and I was going to find out who it was, no matter what. I had to make a plan to help the cops catch the killer. "Hey, Mom, I think I'm going to go to bed. I love you," I said around 8:30 P.M.

"Oh, okay, Hun, but why are you going to bed so early? It's only eight," she asked.

"I'm just tired from the trip and everything that happened. I can't wait to sleep in my own bed," I replied.

"Okay. I love you. Sleep well!" she said as she was making a cup of tea.

I made my way up the stairs to my room. After I closed my door, I sent a group chat to everyone who was in the woods with me. *Hey, guys, do you want to grab a coffee tomorrow and talk about what happened?*

Jess texted back first. *Yes. Nick, can you drive us all to the coffee shop in the morning?*

Sure thing. What time should I pick you guys up? Nick replied around twenty minutes later.

I texted back. *Is 10:00 A.M. good for you guys?*

Everyone agreed, so I turned off my phone and turned on a movie. I woke up around 8:00 A.M. and got into the shower. Nick texted the group about an hour later saying that he was on his way. I wrote my mom a note that I would be at the coffee shop with Nick, Jess, Matthew, and Chase if she got home before me. She usually got home around 1:00 P.M. on workdays. I waited outside for Nick and decided to check if anyone had texted me. Lydia had. *Hey, girl, I just heard about what happened. Are you okay?*

Yeah, I'm fine, I'm just waiting to get interviewed by the cops and everything. I don't know how someone could do that to Sarah, though, I replied.

I mean, I can kind of understand why. She was kinda annoying and stuck up, but like no disrespect, I know y'all used to be close and everything, she texted back.

I didn't think she was. Did you not like her? I texted.

Well, I didn't not like her, but I also didn't like her, you know? she replied.

Yeah, I get it. I just didn't know that, I texted back and turned off my phone as Nick pulled into my driveway. I got in and saw that Chase and Matthew were already in the truck.

"Come on," I said. "We still have to get Jess, and I have a lot to tell you guys."

Nick nodded his head, and we started driving toward Jess's house. I texted her and told her to wait outside because we would be there in a couple of minutes. While I was texting her, I saw that Lydia had texted me again, but I ignored it and turned my phone off. We would all be interrogated the next morning, so I had to ask everyone if they wanted to help the police find out who had killed Sarah. A couple of minutes later, we arrived at Jess's house and picked her up.

"Hey, guys, I was going to wait until we got to the coffee shop to tell you this, but I don't think I can wait. I have a plan to find out who killed Sarah, or at least to help the cops find out who did it," I blurted out.

"Well, the more we can do to help, the better. What's your plan, girl?" Jess asked.

"Yeah, whatever we can do to help, just let us know," Nick and Chase said while Matthew stayed silent.

"Okay, good. Thank you, guys. My plan is to get info for the cops to find out who might've killed Sarah. We'll go around asking random people if they know anyone who didn't like Sarah. Then, we give that list of names to the cops and let them do their own investigation. After that, it's really up to the cops as to what more we can do to help." I breathed out a sigh of relief.

Nick said, "You know, Mary, that's probably the best idea you've come up with in a while."

I rolled my eyes and said, "Oh, shut up. Are you guys in?" I looked around at everyone. We had arrived at the coffee shop while I was talking, and I hadn't even noticed.

Jess said, "Yes, that's actually a good plan," while opening the truck door to get out.

Chase then said, "Yeah, I'm in. I have nothing better to do."

I was so lost in thought that I hadn't noticed that Matthew hadn't said a word the entire trip until Nick pointed it out as we were walking in the coffee shop. He said, "Matthew, are you in? You never said if you were or not."

"Oh, um, yeah, I'm in," he said as we all sat down at the booth.

"Good, we're all in. How have you guys been since everything happened? I've barely been able to sleep since I saw her," I said.

Jess looked up from her menu and said, "Yeah, me neither. I can't believe someone would do that to Sarah. She was genuinely the sweetest girl ever."

"I've been alright, I guess," Matthew said while looking at his menu.

The waitress came around and asked what we would like to drink. After she had left, Nick said, "I've been better. I just wish I could figure out who did this to her."

Sarah, Nick, and I had grown up together in the same neighborhood until I moved across town. We were all super close, but then, Sarah's parents got divorced, and she started getting quieter, hardly ever speaking to us anymore. Then, we just kinda stopped talking all together, aside from the occasional 'Hi.'

"Well," Chase said, "we are helping to find out who killed her, so we and the police should figure it out in no time."

I nodded. "I wonder if it's someone we know," said Jess.

Matthew started choking on his coffee when she said that. He wiped his mouth off and said, "I doubt it, that's crazy."

"I mean, it's not that crazy. There are about two hundred kids in our school, and only about a hundred of them came on the camping trip. We pretty much knew everyone who was there. It'll be pretty easy to narrow the search down," Chase said.

Matthew sat there shaking his head and then got on his phone and started texting someone. We just ignored him because we thought he was probably just upset and didn't know how to process his emotions. We kept talking about who we thought didn't really like Sarah. I felt my phone buzz; my mom had texted me to get her a bagel before I left. That was when I noticed the time.

"Oh shoot, it's 1:00, guys. We'd better start heading home."

"True," Jess said, putting on her coat.

"Before we leave, my mom asked me to get her a bagel, so I'll meet you in the car," I said.

"Okay, Mary, see you in a second," Nick said, putting on his coat.

I went to the counter and asked for the bagel. Once I paid for it, I went outside and climbed into Nick's car.

"We'll drop Jess off first, then you," Nick said.

"Okay," I said as I texted Mom. *I got your bagel. I'll be home in about ten minutes.* I turned my phone off and looked out the window. I wondered why Lydia had been acting so weird. Maybe she was just in shock about Sarah's death and her grief affected her differently. Wait, what if she was the killer? No. No way. She couldn't be. It was crazy for me even to think that way. Well, it would kind of make sense because before Sarah died, she had started dating Lydia's ex, and Lydia was in love with her ex. Still, I didn't think Lydia would kill her over that.

"Mary, we're at your house," Chase said.

"Oh. Sorry. I was in my own world. Bye, guys."

"Bye," everyone said as I was getting out.

I went inside and saw mom sitting on the couch. "Hey, here's your bagel," I said.

"Aw, thank you, Honey. Did you have fun?" she asked.

"Yeah, I went with Chase, Nick, and Jess, and Matthew," I said.

"Oh? Why didn't Lydia go? Didn't you guys used to hang out all the time?" she asked.

"Umm, she said she didn't feel like going out today," I said and then looked at my shoes.

"Oh, okay. Have you talked to her to see how she's doing?"

"Well, she texted me last night to ask if I was okay. She said she was doing alright, but then this morning, she started acting weird, saying she didn't really like Sarah. She said some really bad things about her, which I thought was a little strange."

"That is weird. I wonder why she would do that."

"I know, right? I don't know. I'm going to go to my room. I love you, Mom!"

"Okay, Honey. I love you, too."

I headed back to my room. Jess had texted the group to tell us that Lydia had texted her. I responded immediately, asking what she had said because one, I'm nosy, and two, maybe she was talking bad about Sarah again. About five minutes passed before Jess responded. *Okay, Lydia asked me why we went out and didn't invite her, and I said that we just wanted to talk about how we all were since the incident. Since she wasn't in the woods when we found the body, we didn't think to invite her. Then, Lydia said, 'Oh, okay. Well, who do you think killed Sarah?' I was surprised and said that I didn't know. 'Well, ok, bye,' she said.*

I responded, *I do feel bad about not inviting her, but you are right. We were the ones who found the body. I forgot to tell you guys this morning that she also told me she had never liked Sarah. She's been acting really weird since everything happened.*

Chase finally decided to text. *That's weird. She texted me the same thing.*

Yeah, me, too, Nick replied.

After I finished reading all their texts, I decided to check the text Lydia had sent me earlier in the morning. She had just sent a thumbs-up emoji. Why was Lydia acting like this when she had never said anything bad about Sarah when she was alive?

I texted the group. *Guys, I know this seems kind of crazy, but what if Lydia is the one who killed Sarah? I know we don't have a lot of evidence, but she didn't come to the woods to meet up with us. She's acting really weird, and she has a motive for killing her.*

Matthew was the first to respond. *NO. No way. Lydia would never do anything like that.*

Well, I think Mary is kind of right. I mean she does have a motive, she has been acting weird, and she did not meet us in the woods. She would never miss a group hang out, no matter how tired she was, Chase replied.

Thank you, I texted. *Also, Matthew, we know you've been in love with Lydia for, like, forever, but she seriously could be the killer.* Matthew stopped replying.

Anyway, Jess responded, *I think you're right, Mary. Besides, guys, don't forget that we all have our interrogations tomorrow, so we can bring this up.*

I know, and we have to ask if we can help investigate, Nick replied.

Yes, I texted back, *but for now, we need to gather more evidence to see if Lydia really could be the killer. We don't want to blame murder on someone without the proper amount of evidence.*

True. Well, I have to go. I'll talk to you guys later, Nick texted.

Yeah, same. TTYL, Jess texted back.

Okay, bye, guys. Chase, do you want to help me get info on Lydia? I asked.

Sure, what do I need to do?

Okay, what I need you to do is text some of the guys in our grade and see if they know anything about Lydia not liking Sarah. I'll do the same, but with some of the girls in our grade, I texted, and he sent a thumbs up. I guessed that meant he was going to do it. Then, I had to get to work. I texted a couple of girls in my grade, and they all basically said the same thing, except for one girl who was really close with Lydia. She said that Lydia had joked about wanting to kill Sarah for stealing her ex. I thanked her, then screenshot what she had said. I was about to send it to the group when Chase messaged me privately and sent me a screenshot of someone saying how Matthew and Lydia had been planning something before the field trip.

Do you think Matthew is helping Lydia? Chase asked.

I think he might have something to do with it. Let's send this to everyone in the group except Matthew. We can't have him knowing that we know anything, I texted back.

You're right. I'll send it to everyone.

Okay. Here is a screenshot of what one of Lydia's friends said. I'm going to send this to everyone as well, I texted.

Yeah, I really think she's the one who did it now, Chase replied.

Yes, I texted back, then heard a knock on my door. "Come in!" I yelled.

My mom opened the door and said, "Are you okay, honey? You've been in your room for five hours."

"Oh, yeah, I'm fine; I've just been watching some TV."

"Okay. Well, dinner's almost ready," she said while walking out of my room.

"I'll be down in a minute. I love you, Mom."

"I love you, too, Sweetie."

I went downstairs a couple of minutes after I sent the screenshot to everyone and saw that Mom had made my favorite food. "What's this for?" I asked while sitting down at the table.

"Well, I just thought you should eat something good because you have a big day tomorrow," she said, handing me a bowl of my favorite soup.

"Yeah, I guess. Thanks, Mom," I said.

A little while later, I went back to my room, changed into my pajamas, and turned on a movie. It had been taking me a while to fall asleep ever since the field trip. Around two hours later, I finally fell asleep. I woke up the next morning to the sound of my alarm. This was the day. I changed clothes. My mom was waiting for me downstairs.

"Are you ready to go?" she asked.

"Yeah, let's go," I answered. I checked my phone once we got into the car and saw that I had been added to a group chat with Nick, Chase, and Jess last night. I decided I would check the messages when I got back home. As we started parking at the police station, I saw everyone else already inside.

"I'll see you later, Mom. I'll text you when you should come pick me up."

"Okay, Honey, I love you!" she said.

When I got inside, I signed in, then went to join my friends.

"Hey, guys," I said quietly.

"Hey, Mary. They told us they'd be ready for us shortly. I'm pretty sure they said they wanted to talk to you first since you were the first one to see the body," Nick said, looking at me anxiously. I could tell he was scared. He'd been scared of getting in trouble since we were little.

"That makes sense—" I said before being cut off.

"Mary Davis?" a lady with a clipboard said.

"Right here," I said, walking towards her.

"Follow me, please," she said, then led me down the hallway. My heart was pounding. I'd never been inside a police station before. We stopped at a door near the end of the hallway, and she told me to go inside and sit down; a detective would be in shortly. I sat and waited. It was cold inside the room. A little while later, a woman with brown hair in a tight bun came in. She was wearing a black suit.

"Hello Mary, I'm Detective Lopez. I have a couple of questions for you, and then you'll be free to go," she said as she held out her hand.

I shook it and said, "Hi."

"Okay, the first question: How close were you to the victim?"

"Well, Sarah and I grew up together. We were really close until a couple of months ago when she started pushing everyone away." I looked at my shoes.

"Okay, next question: Do you know of anyone who had a problem with the victim?" She was writing in a notebook.

"Kind of? My best friend, Lydia Jones. I never thought she had a problem with Sarah, but lately, she'd been acting weird and talking bad about her."

"Okay, last question," she said while pulling something out of the brown box next to her. "Do you know if Lydia wears bracelets that look like this?" She pulled out a small bag with a broken bracelet inside. I looked at it closely and gasped.

"Yes! She and I have matching friendship bracelets. We never take them off."

"Interesting. So, do you, by any chance, know how she lost it if she never took it off?" she asked condescendingly.

"No, I don't. Did you find it near the tents or in the lunchroom at the campsite?" I thought Lydia might have just misplaced it. But how could she have gone this long without saying anything about losing the bracelet? I mean, I wouldn't have been mad, but I would have wanted to know.

"We found it by the body. Mary, do you know why Lydia was anywhere near that body? Could someone have planted the bracelet there?"

"No, Lydia wasn't there when my friends and I went to the woods. I figured she just fell asleep early. Besides, look, I have mine on right now." I lifted my arm so she could see my bracelet.

"Thank you, Ms. Davis, you may be dismissed."

As I walked out, I heard the office calling Nick. I decided to wait with Matthew, Jess, and Chase.

"So, what did she ask you?" Jess asked.

"She asked about Lydia because they found her bracelet."

"Wait, what do you mean they found her bracelet? She wasn't with us. Why would her bracelet be there?" Chase said.

"I don't know, but I think we were right about Lydia, at least partly."

Chase butted in, whispering, "Guys, I know you want to talk about this, but Matthew is like right there."

"Oh yeah, I forgot about Matt. I'll text you the rest." I promised.

"Won't he wonder why we're not talking? What if he asks what they asked you?" asked Jess.

"Okay I'll tell him that they asked how close Sarah and I were, and what we were doing in the woods," I replied quietly. Just then, Nick came out. Chase was called to take his place. After the police had questioned each one of us, we told them our plan to help them find the killer. Surprisingly, they accepted the offer, but we had to report to them immediately if we found anything. We agreed, and Nick and Chase left. I texted my mom to pick me up. Jess got picked up a few minutes later, leaving Matthew and me alone outside.

"So, who do you think did it?" he asked while looking down at his phone.

"Huh?" I was confused.

"I mean, who do you think the killer is?" he asked as he turned off his phone and looked at me.

Something was off. I didn't know what it was, but something deep inside told me not to say or do anything stupid. "I don't know," I answered and shrugged my shoulders. I went back to looking at my phone to see how far away my mom was. Matthew was staring at me; I could feel it.

"You don't think it's Lydia anymore?" he asked.

I continued staring at my phone. "Well, it was just a thought that popped into my head. You were right, it was stupid to think Lydia could be the killer. She would never do something like that." I turned to look at him. He just nodded and looked back at his phone. I started to text the group when my mom pulled into the parking lot. Without even looking at Matthew, I walked to the car.

"Hey, Sweetie, how was it?" my mom asked.

"The actual questioning wasn't bad, but Matthew was acting so weird out there," I told her.

"I'm sorry, Honey. At least the questioning wasn't bad."

I nodded and then checked my phone. I decided it was finally time to see what the group was talking about.

Okay, we've all seen what Lydia and Matthew have been saying. What do you all think about it? Chase had texted.

I think if Lydia did kill Sarah, she didn't do it alone. There's no way that little five-foot-tall Lydia could kill Sarah, who was at least six inches taller, Jess replied.

That's true. If anyone helped her, it would have been Matthew. He would do anything for her. And his love probably blinded him a little too much this time, Nick responded.

Honestly, I think we just solved the murder, Jess texted. Nick and Chase did not reply.

I finally texted back. *Guys, I agree. I think we solved it. We just need more evidence on Matthew, and then, we can tell the cops.*

Nick and Chase sent thumbs up, and Jess replied, *True, but how can we connect Matthew to the murder?*

I don't know, but as long as we bring Lydia down, she'll bring down everyone who helped her, I texted back.

We decided each of us would talk to Lydia, since she had asked us what was going on and why we weren't texting anymore in the group chat. With all the investigating we were doing, I had forgotten that we were texting in another group chat. We sent screenshots of what Lydia texted to each of us, and Jess realized she would change her story each time she texted us. For example, when she texted me, she asked why we hadn't been texting in the group anymore and admitted that she felt left out; but when she texted Nick, she asked why we weren't texting in the group anymore but then asked if it was because we weren't friends anymore. She kept asking each person different questions, as if she were trying to get as much information as possible. A couple of days later, when we felt we had collected enough information to pin the murder on Lydia, we decided to take it to the cops.

"Are you guys ready?" Nick asked us outside the police station.

"As ready as we'll ever be," I said back.

As we walked inside, I couldn't stop thinking about how our evidence could possibly put Lydia away for the rest of her life. My best friend was a murderer. My life was going to change drastically. So would hers. When we got to the front desk, we asked for the detective who had first asked us about the murder.

We were invited to take seats in the waiting area, and I started to cry. Detective Lopez came over as I wiped away my tears.

"You wanted to see me?" she asked, sitting down in front of us.

"Yes, we have some evidence that Lydia Jones may have killed Sarah," I stated.

Detective Lopez stopped and stared at us for what seemed like ages. "Come with me, all of you. I have something to show you." She took us to a small room in the back of the station and pulled out a box labeled 'Campsite Murder.' Inside were a couple of bags, and a folder filled with paperwork.

"What is this?" Nick asked.

"It's all evidence that Lydia is our killer," Lopez said. "Please give me your phones so my team and I can collect all the evidence. We'll only go through your messages with Lydia."

I was the first to hand her my phone and give her my password. Then Jess. Then Nick. And finally, Chase. The detective thanked us and told us to remain in the waiting area. A couple of hours later, she returned and gave us back our phones. She said that Lydia would be arrested, and we should go home. Nick said he could drive since it was late and we didn't want to wake our parents.

"It's still crazy that I'm the only one in the group who has my license," Nick said, trying to cheer us up.

"Oh, be quiet, you're also the oldest in our grade," I said, smiling.

He smiled back and then looked at the road. I turned around to see what Jess and Chase were doing. They had fallen asleep. I didn't blame them; I was tired, too. When I got home, my mom was waiting for me in the living room. I sat down next to her and started crying. All at once it hit me: I would never be able to hang out with Lydia again. I might not be able to even see her again. My mom hugged me, and I fell asleep in her arms. When I woke up later, I checked my texts. Lydia had confessed to everything, and Matthew had helped her. We had found the killer. Finally, this nightmare was over.

***

Two Years Later

We're seniors now. Jess, Nick, Chase, and I are still pretty close, but it's weird without Matt and Lydia. I fell into a pretty deep depression not long after Lydia was sentenced. Junior year was hard, but I got through it with a little help from my family and friends. Lydia received life in prison; Matt was given thirty years. I visit them from time to time to see how they're doing. It's still crazy that two years ago, I put my best friends away for murder. We're graduating in three months. I plan to major in criminal justice, Jess is going to be a doctor, Chase dropped out last year to work at his dad's company, and Nick is going to join the army. I miss Lydia and Matt sometimes, but I'm happy that we were able to get justice for Sarah and her mom.

Perfect

By Brittney Napier

Rose Jackson, a thirteen-year-old girl, had always been a straight-A student, even though she had many problems with her health. She had Down syndrome, ADHD, asthma problems, and dyslexia, but she played the sport she loved: soccer! Ever since she was little, she loved soccer, and she had always been really good at it. She played for Mabry County Junior High. Rose had always been the best player on the team though she had always thought she was the worst. That was the mindset Rose had: Everything had to be better because nothing could ever be perfect.

The day started as a normal day: waking up, getting ready, and then going to school. Rose went to all of her classes, and it was finally the end of the day. She had the worst locker on the opposite end of the hallway from all her classes. As she hurried down the hallway trying to get to the locker room to get ready for her game, she ran into Matthew Jones, her best friend, who was the nicest and cutest boy in the entire school with his blond hair, icy blue eyes, and perfect face. Rose looked up at him, embarrassed, and blurted out, "I'm so sorry! I'm just in a rush to get to the locker room!"

Matthew smiled and replied, "It's fine; don't worry about it. Want to walk with me?" He held out his hand for her to take.

Rose smiled and nodded, but as soon as she was about to grab his hand, her asthma kicked in because she was so nervous about holding his hand. Matthew looked at her. He was confused at first and then realized what was happening. "Oh my gosh..."

Rose wheezed as she went through her bag trying to find her inhaler. Matthew took her bag and dumped everything out on the hallway floor. Binders, books, highlighters, erasers, and chewed-up pencils went everywhere. Then, at the very bottom of her bag, her blue inhaler fell onto the ground. Matthew threw the bag down, grabbed her inhaler, and put it up to her mouth. "Breathe...take deep breaths. In...out...in...out," he said while rubbing her back, trying to help her catch her breath.

After a while, Rose started to breathe normally. "Thanks," she mumbled. She began to pick up her things and put them back in her bag. "Lucky you were here...If not, I probably would have passed out."

Matthew laughed a little. "Yeah, you would've had to wait until our principal walked down the hallway."

She laughed and smiled. "That would've been horrible!"

Matthew held out his hand again and helped her up. "Yeah! I don't think anyone likes that lady! She's the worst! Now, maybe you can make it to the locker room without dying!" Rose took his hand, trying not to be nervous because she didn't want to have another asthma attack.

As the two walked down the hallway, they ran into Mr. Markel. He stopped and stared at them for a moment before speaking up. "Rose, are you doing ok?" Before Rose could respond, Mr. Markel continued, "You look really pale. I heard noises outside of my classroom sounding like hyperventilating and wheezing."

She looked at Mr. Markel. "Y-yeah, I'm perfectly fine," she mumbled.

Matthew looked at Rose like she was crazy and yelled out, "She, in fact, is not fine! She just had an asthma attack!"

Mr. Markel, who was not just the English teacher, but also the coach of the soccer team, looked at Rose with concern and said, "Rose, do you need to skip the game tonight?"

Rose exclaimed, "No! No! No! I'm fine! Matthew doesn't know what he is talking about!" She shoved her bag into Matthew's arms and gave him a glare that said, "Shut up before I punch the snot out of you."

Matthew rolled his eyes and gave her a look back that said, "You're not fine, though!" Mr. Markel just stood there looking as confused as a kangaroo in the Himalayan Mountains!

He shook his head. "I don't believe you're fine! I'm calling your dad to come pick you up right now."

Matthew pulled out his phone. "There is no need to call her dad. My mom can take her home. I mean, we are neighbors."

Rose sighed, grumbled, then nodded. "I'll just text my dad we're going to hang out or whatever."

Mr. Markel nodded as Rose pulled out her phone and started typing aggressively. A few seconds later, her phone dinged. "My dad said that was fine, and he isn't going to be home until really late. I would've had come to your house after my game anyway."

Matthew nodded, "So does that mean you're just going to sleep over at my house or...?"

Rose looked at him like he was the dumbest person who had ever set foot on the planet. "Well, you know my dad would never let me stay home alone. He thinks I would get kidnapped or burn the house down trying to make mac & cheese. Though it wasn't my fault when the mac & cheese fire started! It was yours! I told you not to leave the mac & cheese on because we were going outside. But, of course, you had to leave it on." Rose rolled her eyes. "Whatever. I'm getting off-topic. I will just have to get my medication and other inhalers." Matthew looked guilty as charged knowing that the so-called 'mac & cheese fire' was his fault.

Matthew's mom's car pulled up, and they both waved at Mr. Markel. "Bye, Coach Markel!" Rose yelled as they got in the car.

She looked at Matthew's mom. "Hi, Mrs. Jones! Thanks for picking me up from school."

Mrs. Jones smiled. "How many times have I said you can call me Mom?"

Matthew blurted out, "I call you Mom all the time, and you never have to tell me to!"

She turned around to look at Rose and Matthew in the backseat. "Matthew, you call me Mom because I am your mother. Rose doesn't because I'm not her mother," she said, annoyed, as she rolled her eyes and started the car.

Rose pulled out her math homework to do as they went home, and Matthew did the same. Rose sighed, "Why do we always have so much homework every night? We have like a bajillion math problems to do tonight! I wish just one time we wouldn't have homework!" She pouted.

Matthew looked at her and laughed. "Yeah, but she only gave us, like, three problems tonight!" He looked down at his homework.

Rose gave him a death glare. "Yeah, yeah, whatever! Wait, don't we have to start reading some kind of chapter book tomorrow in English for like a book report or something?" She frowned as she looked back at her homework.

"Yeah, why?" Matthew looked up from his homework. He was confused.

Rose stared at him for a few seconds, and the light bulb went off in his head. "Oh...that probably won't go too well for you, huh? Shouldn't they have some kind of alternative assignment or have someone read the book to you?"

Rose continued to stare at her homework, "Yeah, they should, but they won't. You know they don't care! As long as I don't die in the class, they don't care what grade I make."

Mrs. Jones turned into the driveway and pulled the car into the garage. "Ok, we're here! I'm going to make dinner. You two need to finish your homework before doing anything else."

Rose and Matthew both replied, "Yes, Mom!"

Rose grabbed her red, white, and blue soccer bag, then her regular bag, and got out of the car. Matthew grabbed his bag and followed her inside. They both threw their bags down and sat down next to each other to do homework. Matthew groaned, "Ugh! So much homework!"

Rose glared at him because when she said the amount of homework they had was outrageous, Matthew said it wasn't that bad. Matthew sunk down in his chair, "Um... Hahaha! Maybe we do have a bunch of homework."

Rose kept glaring and grumbled, "Really? You think so?"

Sweat ran down Matthew's face. "I'm sorry! I didn't mean to make you mad." Rose's expression went blank, and he couldn't tell her what she was thinking. Matthew was bracing himself as he waited for Rose to punch him.

Rose's expression turned to confusion as she opened her mouth to say something, but instead of talking, she just closed her mouth. Then, she got up, walked to the bathroom, and locked herself in. Matthew just sat there in silence, the only noise was the clock ticking. He felt super awkward. All of a sudden, he heard a loud crash coming from the bathroom. He ran to the bathroom and banged on the door, screaming, "ROSE! ARE YOU OK? ROSE! ROSE!" He finally heard the lock click, and the door opened. Rose was on the floor about to pass out. She had her head in her hands. Matthew's expression turned to horror as he saw her ADHD bottle was empty. "Wait, so you ran out of pills but didn't say anything about getting more on the way home?"

Rose looked up at him. "I forgot. That's the effect of ADHD; you should know that. I was going to say something and then forgot what I was going to say."

Matthew sighed, "Why didn't you just get the bottle out before? Also, why the heck are you on the floor?!"

Rose looked up at him again. "That is the problem! I forgot! Also, you know I get tired if I don't take my medicine."

Matthew looked down at her and asked the last question she would've expected: "You know, why do you always act so weird around me?"

Rose looked away, her face turning red. She never admitted it before, but she liked Matthew. Not as a friend, though. Like, she had a massive crush on him, but little did she know, he liked her back. Both of them were just too shy to tell each other. Rose smiled, blushed, and looked back down at the floor. "I don't know what you're talking about. I've never been weird around you!"

Matthew lifted her chin up and looked into her eyes, his face even redder than hers. "Well...I...um...I...I...I want to tell you something." Rose continued to stare into his eyes waiting for him to talk. He gulped and yelled out, "I like you! I like you as more than a friend!" His face looked like the shiny red apple Mr. Markel had on his desk every morning. Rose turned away smiling and blushing. Matthew opened his mouth and tried to talk, but no words came out. They just stared at each other in awkward silence for a few minutes.

Matthew kept blushing and finally spoke up. "I want to ask you something, but I don't know how to say it." He gulped and took a deep breath. "I know you probably don't like me back, and I've already told you I like you." He laughed nervously, wiping the sweat off his palms. "I know you were upset because you had missed the championship game because of me. I know you're mad at me, and I'm sorry. I was just worried something would hap–"

Rose covered his mouth with her hand. "I like you, too. I've always liked you. I was just scared to admit it. I thought you could never like someone like me."

Matthew continued, "Well, let me ask you this now–do you want to be my girlfriend?" He flashed his cheesy smile.

Rose gasped. This is what she had always wanted! She had dreamed of this day since they met! She smiled, "Of course, I want to be your girlfriend! You're, like, the sweetest person I've ever met! Girls and maybe a few boys would die to be with you!" Matthew smiled and took her hand. He was about to say something, but she put her finger over his mouth. "Now we need to finish math homework so we both don't fail!" They laughed together.

About a week later, it was almost time for them to move up to eighth grade. As the days, weeks, and months went by, they stayed a happy couple. Even when they got to high school, they were a couple. Though this all started with an asthma attack, they were truly meant to be the perfect couple.

Merriwether Money

By Levi Ramsey

Part 1

Matthew Livingston had a pretty troubled life throughout his fourteen years. His father was a farmhand and an alcoholic who beat his wife, and his mother was a waitress with barely any money. One day, Matthew's mother decided she was tired of getting beaten and left, leaving him with his father. This threw Matthew into a depression. However, it made his father angry. Soon enough, Matthew's father started beating him. After one too many beatings, Matthew had enough. He went behind the house, grabbed a shovel, walked back in, and smacked his father on the forehead, knocking him to the ground. That made his father even more angry. So, his father took off on his horse and didn't return. Just like that, Matthew was completely on his own. He wanted to get a job, but nobody would hire him. Eventually, he turned to a life of crime.

One day, he was caught stealing from the general store. A man smoking a cigar was leaning against the small brick building. The store owner took Matthew outside to find his parents, but the cigar smoker was the only one standing outside. The shop owner asked the man if he was Matthew's father, and for some reason, he said yes. Matthew had no choice but to go with the man, so he climbed onto the back of the man's horse. It turns out that the man was a gang leader. Once he and Matthew arrived at camp, he introduced himself. His name was Thomas Ramon. The gang was made up of six people, including the leader: Jose Santez, James Fuqua, Kinsley Barnes, John Dyer, and Brody Banks. They had just arrived in the state of Kansas, and had heard that the richest bank was there. They couldn't pass up an opportunity that big. There was one big problem, however: They didn't have enough resources. They would have to do what they do best: be criminals.

Where they were staying was abundant in gold. This gave Thomas an idea. If the place was filled with gold, he was sure that there would be some big mining companies; and if they pulled it off just right, they could catch them selling their gold and rob them. First, though, they had to have a plan, so Matthew and Brody were sent to scope out the situation. They pulled into town and began asking questions, beginning in the saloon. They came across a feeble old man who was bald just on the top of his head. Brody asked him if he knew of any big mining companies in the area. He replied "Of course. Have you not heard of the Millers? They're not really a company, but more of a family. Still, they mine gold and sell it, so I don't see much of a difference."

"Well," Brody asked, "what do you know about them?"

"I know they mine somewhere near Welch Plains," the old man responded.

"What time are they usually out there?" Brody asked.

"Oh, I don't know that much", the old man replied.

Brody thanked him for his time and left. He and Matthew had what they needed, except the time. They went back to camp to report to Thomas. He was pleased with the information, but he needed to know about the time. He spent some time thinking and soon came up with a plan: He would send his two smallest and quietest men out to Welch Plains, where the old man had said the mine was. Then, they would ask around and find out where the Millers kept their sales records. They would camp there until night, when no one would see them. While one broke into the office, the other would keep a lookout.

By the next morning, Thomas had decided whom he wanted to send. He called Matthew and James over to his tent. "You two will be going to scope out the Miller Mining Company. This job needs to be handled very secretly. We can't get caught. If we do, the whole job will be a bust, do y'all got that?"

Of course, James and Matthew agreed. The two boys were not chosen at random. Thomas had his reasons. First, he chose Matthew because he was the smallest and, therefore, the quietest and quickest of Thomas' men. He chose James because he was undoubtedly the sneakiest one in the group; there wasn't a single person he couldn't get by.

***

Part 2

Before setting out for Welch Plains, Matthew needed a way to get around. People were tired of giving him rides. He was just a teenager with barely any money, so if he wanted a horse, he would have to steal one. He talked to James about it. James asked Matthew if he had any breed in mind. Matthew told him that he loved American Paints. He had wanted one ever since he was little because his grandpa had had one. Since American Paints were mainly from Canada, they would be hard to find in Kansas. Nonetheless, James and Matthew headed over to the stables in town and asked the owner if he had any.

"This is your lucky day," the man replied. He had one. Matthew and James looked at the horse, and it was perfect. It was mostly brown with a white face. Matthew had to act quickly. He couldn't come back that night to steal it because he would be breaking into the mining office. Since he couldn't wait any longer, he pulled out the old revolver that Thomas had given him and threatened to shoot if the owner of the stables didn't give him the horse and a saddle right then. The man had no choice but to hand over what Matthew wanted. Matthew promised that if he told anybody about what had just transpired, he wouldn't live to see the next sunrise.

It was getting late, so James and Matthew decided to set up camp. They found a spot and then split up. They acted like it was their first day on the job with the Millers and began asking questions about the sales records. They wrote down what they found out. The records were kept in the company office, and they found out where it was. Once it got very dark, they reunited and headed over to the office. There was a slight problem, though: Guards were everywhere. It would be difficult to go any farther. The door was locked, so one of them would have to find another way in while the other stood watch. James said he would climb through a window, but as soon as he reached the office, a guard appeared. James lied. He told the guard that he was a new employee and that he was lost, but the guard wasn't falling for it. James knocked him out with the butt of his gun and hid him in the bushes underneath the window. Then, he climbed into the house and looked all over until he found the room with the sales records. While Matthew was standing guard, he peeked through the window and saw somebody standing behind the door. As soon as James walked in, the person started choking him. Panicked, Matthew leaped through the open window and fired his revolver. The assailant fell to the ground, but he wasn't dead. While Matthew promised to finish him off if he screamed, James searched through the sales records until he found what he was looking for. He scribbled down the time for the next meeting; then, he and Matthew climbed out the window and hustled back to camp. They didn't want any more trouble than they had already had.

***

Part 3

They gave Thomas the information they had collected. He looked it over. The next sales meeting was to be held on Friday, the very next day. When the gang woke up that morning, Thomas told them how the job would be done. Everyone understood and headed out to the wagon crossing. The six men were broken up into groups of two: Matthew and Jose, Kinsley and Brody, and John and James. Thomas would meet the leader of the wagons. They spread out to hide. Once the wagons arrived, Thomas told the guards to drop their weapons. Of course, they didn't listen and threatened to shoot. Thomas gave the signal, and the gang members ambushed the wagons and started firing. After a couple of guards were shot, the others ran away to get the police. Thomas made the wagon drivers open the chests filled with gold and released them. They promised not to say a word about what had happened. Thomas and his men quickly stowed all that they could in their sacks and on their horses and returned to camp to count their loot. Thomas sent James to find a buyer. When he returned, Kinsley and Matthew joined him to meet the buyer. They negotiated a deal and walked away with two thousand dollars, more than enough to fund their robbery of the Merriwether bank.

∗∗∗

Part 4

The men split some of the money for themselves, and Thomas took what was left. He put everybody to work to get ready to rob the bank. When the appointed day came, they all got their guns, put on their masks, headed over to the bank, and went in. Then, James and Brody pointed their guns at the guards and told them to drop their weapons. Kinsley and John kept guard, and Thomas held the bank teller at gunpoint and made him open the vault. Jose and Matthew went in, but they didn't know there was another guard inside the vault. Jose was shot. Matthew quickly turned around and shot the guard two times with his repeater. He died immediately. Matthew wasn't worried about the money at that point; he had to check on Jose. He hoped that he wasn't dead, but sure enough, when he knelt by his motionless partner, he saw Jose with a bullet hole in his forehead. There was nothing he could do. Jose was dead. He took Jose's sack and filled it up with all that he could and walked out of the vault. The police were waiting for him. Matthew scrambled around the bank looking for a way that the gang could escape, but with every door and window covered by the police, it seemed there was no way to escape.

The Break Up

By Callie Rose, Emery Gammon, and Khloe Wilson

I was in a toxic relationship with the person I believed to be my high school sweetheart. I thought it was true love, but I was completely wrong. Our relationship was rough, and there was always a problem with him. I could usually let it slide, until finally he did something unforgivable. Now, I am with the love of my life, Gabriel, who will always be there for me – unlike Henry, the high school sweetheart. I regretted my high school years until I met Gabriel during my junior year of high school.

Henry and I had been together for six years. I had known him since third grade, and thought that he was the sweetest, kindest person that I had ever met. When Henry and I started dating in fifth grade, he called me Ell, even though my name was Eleanor. I thought it was the best nickname. Henry and I would text, call, and hang out every weekend when we were in the seventh grade. When we got to high school, everyone and everything changed.

That's when he slowly started drifting away from me. We stayed together because it seemed that other people wanted us to. But in the middle of October of our freshman year of high school, we started to have many problems, such as Henry ignoring me for long periods of time.

Going home wasn't great, either, because my parents were in the middle of a divorce. They always involved me in their arguments. Even our dinners were horrible, because we would just sit in silence and look around the room. For example, on my fifteenth birthday, my mom cooked green peas, mashed potatoes, macaroni and cheese, and rolls. This was my favorite dinner. We all sat down for dinner, and the only thing that my parents said was, "Happy birthday, Kiddo." My dad, Dalton Jane, wouldn't eat, and my mom, Sarah Jane, just played with her food. I was the only person actually enjoying my meal. After sitting in silence for a while, my mom got up to get my birthday cake out of the refrigerator. She grabbed some paper plates out of the cabinet next to the fridge and set them on the table, along with the cake. She handed me a slice of cake, and I sat in excitement, waiting for my parents to sing "Happy Birthday" to me. However, they helped themselves to the cake and kept silent. After dinner, I went to my room and cried because they didn't seem to care that it was my birthday. I will never forget that day, and the fact that my birthdays haven't been, and never will be, the same again.

The only good part of my life were my friends, even though they could sometimes be horrible. They involved me in all their personal and school drama. It just reminded me of home. The only person that I thought I could count on was drifting away. I couldn't be distracted from all of this commotion around me, so I started failing some of my classes. I just couldn't focus. I had tried many things, such as being in a room alone, studying, and even getting a tutor. But none of it helped. Not any of it.

I had tried so many times to be at Henry's football games, or even just to contact him, but he was always too busy for me. I never imagined it would be this way, dealing with my parents' divorce, and Henry always busy with football. Once football season was over, Henry had a little more time on his hands, and we could finally spend time together. I was so happy I could get out of the house to see him instead of being at home with my parents.

***

Later, during my sophomore year, Henry and I continued going out. However, he always had somewhere to be, and when I went over to his house and found him at home, he was always on the phone with other people. When Henry and I were on a date one night at The Modern, one of the fanciest restaurants in the city, he stood up, and I asked him where he was going. He just stood there with a blank look on his face, saying nothing and acting like he was stunned by my question. He sat back down with the same face, not saying anything, until the waitress brought us our food. Then, he said, "I'm sorry."

"Why?" I responded.

Then, he said, "For being so distant lately and not making time for you." I was shocked he had apologized. Now the tables had turned, and I was the one stunned into silence.

***

That summer, my parents finally decided to take their divorce to court, and my mom got custody of me. It was the happiest day of my life. It was finally over; there would be no more fighting and arguing. The only downside of the divorce was that my dad left, and I have not seen him since the court day. When the judge began trying the case, Henry was nowhere to be found. I looked everywhere for him, but I just couldn't find him. I tried to call and text him, but there was no response. Later, I found out that he was out with Olivia Hesson – his other girlfriend, the one I had no idea about. I was so furious that I couldn't hold back from instantly breaking up with him.

***

Finally, junior year began. When I walked into school, I saw Gabriel, the new guy. I didn't think much of him until I went to my first class: history. He was there, in the seat right next to mine. He knew the answers to all the questions. Since I didn't understand history class that much, I asked him for help. Once a few weeks had gone by, he asked me on a date to The Modern, the place where Henry had apologized a couple of days before we had broken up. I didn't say anything about that because I didn't want to bring up Henry. I ended up agreeing to the date, and was very excited to go. Gabriel was so nice; he paid for my dinner. After we finished eating, we went to the movies. We watched *Smile 2*, the new horror movie everyone was talking about.

Waiting in line for concessions, we saw Henry and Olivia. My heart sank. "No way they're here at the same time as Gabriel and I. There's no way," I thought. I looked up at Gabriel and saw him looking down at me.

"Something wrong?" he asked as he saw the concern on my face.

I said, "Nothing."

We got popcorn, M&M's, Watermelon Sour Patch Kids, and a large Dr. Pepper. We sat down to watch the movie. I drank almost all of the Dr. Pepper. Later, I had to go to the restroom, and that's when I bumped into Henry. We just stood there, looking at each other; then, out of nowhere, here came Olivia. She looked at me with a disgusted face and pulled Henry into their theater from the lobby. After the movie, Gabriel took me home.

***

One month later, I got a text from Henry. *Eleanor, please meet me at City Park at 1:30 pm.* I decided to go, after what had happened at the theater. Once I got there, he was standing under the pink willow tree, which was one of my favorites.

"Sorry," he said, and I walked over to him and asked him why he had texted me.

Again, he said, "I'm sorry. Me and Olivia are done, and I still have feelings for you. Can we give it another chance?"

I stood there with a shocked look on my face. I was not expecting that. I turned him down, and he asked me why. I told him I was in a months-long relationship with Gabriel Banks. I started to walk off, but Henry stopped me and said, "Wait! He doesn't love you like I love you!" I turned around and then walked away.

***

I told Gabriel everything that had happened, and he didn't know what to say except, "Let me deal with it." A few days later, I overheard a conversation that Gabriel and Henry were having. They were arguing over whether Henry should be allowed to talk to me while I waited outside the door to my English class. It was a very intense conversation, and I thought about butting in a couple of times. Instead, I decided it would be better for them to work it out. I walked away.

***

That night, I blocked Henry on every social media platform and even blocked his phone number on my cell phone so he could not contact me at all. In the hallways at school, Henry tried to talk to me, but I acted like I did not hear him. He even went so far as to try to get my friends to tell me something for him, but when my friends tried to approach me, I told them I did not want to hear what he had to say and walked off.

Once Henry gave up on us, he said that he was not going to be bothering me anymore. I threw my hands up in excitement and ran off to tell Gabriel the good news. He was even more excited than I was because he and I could now be a happy couple. A year had gone by, and my nightmare-like senior year was over. Gabriel and I had made it through all the madness and stayed a happy couple. I am about to move away for college now, and Gabriel and I are both going to the same school: Columbia University.

Shipwreck

By Troy Sepulona and Brody Wohlgamuth

As Amir woke up from a good night's sleep on the cruise ship, he stretched and said, "Good morning," as he passed one of the ship's attendants heading to the cafeteria. He asked for his usual breakfast: a scrambled eggs and two slices of crispy bacon.

While he was eating, Alfred, one of Amir's friends, asked, "What are you eating? The usual?"

"Yeah," Amir replied, "just some eggs and bacon."

"Me, too. Eating, and thinking about my wife back home."

"Yeah," Amir said, "I've been thinking about my wife back home, too."

***

The day went on, and Amir wasn't busy. He couldn't think of anything to do, so he went to swim in the ship's pool. Then, he saw his friends playing basketball, so he decided to join them. Once he arrived, he sat on the bleachers , waiting for his friends Jackson, Joe, Will, and Joan, who were in the middle of a game. When the game ended, Amir asked if he could join.

"I don't mind. You can join if you want," Joe said as he went to grab another ball.

"Me neither," Joan replied. "You can join if you want."

Since none of his friends minded if Amir joined, he began playing. He started scoring basket after basket, but he soon grew tired because he was running up and down the court. So, he decided to get lunch.

While heading to the cafeteria, Amir remembered that today's special was his favorite: smoked tuna and a salad. Since most people did not like smoked tuna, it wasn't very busy in the dining area. Yet, there was one other person, Josh, who Amir knew was also eating. Amir decided to sit with him while having his lunch.

"Hey, Josh," Amir began, "whatcha doing?"

Josh answered, "Hey. I've not been up to much, but have you heard about the storm that's supposed to come through?"

"Yeah," replied Amir, "I heard it's supposed to be pretty bad, but I gotta go." Then, he said, "I'll see you later."

Soon, Amir realized that the storm had begun to rage terribly, and the boat started to rock like a cradle. Little did he know it was going to become much worse.

***

The worst possible thing then happened: The ship started sinking! "JOE! WHERE ARE YOU?" Amir screamed. While the boat was filling up with water, babies were crying, and everybody was panicking. "JOE, WHERE ARE YOU?" Amir cried again just as he was being gripped by fear and panic. Amir was scared. He began to worry that everyone on board would be killed, so he began searching for his friends.

As the night wore on, the boat kept sinking. Just as Amir thought that he and the other passengers might be rescued, he spotted a wave in the distance that was as large as a football field. "Why, God? Why do you have to make it storm now?" Amir cried out, unable to take his eyes off the approaching wave.

The wave seemed to increase in speed as it approached the sinking ship! Amir decided just to give up and sit on the floor. While waiting for the wave to hit, he asked himself, "Why did I want to come on this trip?" He took one final glance at the ocean. Then, the wave struck the ship, and Amir blacked out.

***

"Where am I? What happened to the boat?" Amir asked as he woke up on an island with no one in sight. He could hear all sorts of birds chirping. "The boat," he thought, "must've completely sunk." He had no idea about what to do, but he decided to start trying to build a shelter. While looking around for some sticks, he stumbled upon a swamp that smelled like a wet dog with the slightest hint of salty coconut.

"AHHHHHHHHH!" Amir screamed as a strange-looking dog licked the back of his leg. The only thing that made this dog different was his fur. Instead of having the normal soft fur, he had thick, rough fur.

Amir continued wandering through the forest with his new pal, which he decided to name Rufus. Once he realized that time was running out for him to work on his shelter, he decided to sleep under a big oak log that was leaning against a boulder. Soon, he heard something snapping twigs in the swamp to his left.

Amir peeked around the corner of the boulder to look more closely at the swamp, but then he saw a seven-foot-tall, hairy beast that was feasting on an animal that looked like a rotten cow. Amir ran and hid inside a huge decaying log, and Rufus ran the other way.

***

Early the next morning, Amir was starving. Luckily, there was a bird's nest a couple of branches up. He decided to hit the branch with a long stick, hoping the nest would fall. Once the nest fell, he discovered its few eggs were too old to eat. Amir scavenged through the eggs but found nothing edible. Unlike the ones back home, these eggs were blue and orange.

Although he hated the thought, Amir ate the raw eggs. "UHH!" he gagged the second the slimy yolk touched his tongue. "RUFUS!" he screamed as Rufus ate the other three eggs.

***

A couple of days later, Amir noticed Rufus was growing really fast and eating a lot. Amir had begun thinking that Rufus may not be a dog because of his fur and the rate he was growing. Suddenly, it dawned on him that Rufus was a bear!

***

Amir finally started to exercise his building expertise, and Rufus helped him hunt and fish. Unfortunately, Amir began to get sick. He threw up all day and night. Nonetheless, Rufus continued hunting and fishing for him most of the days. When he wasn't hunting, he was making sure Amir was safe.

Once Amir had recuperated and stopped rolling around under the old, leaning tree, he set off to continue exploring the island. "RUFUS!" he screamed when he saw his companion running around the corner covered in mud. "Hey, Bud, where have you been?" Amir asked.

While exploring, Amir heard the loudest hiss. It wasn't from a snake, though; it was from a big cat lying in the brush. SNAP! Amir stepped on a stick running away from the cat. Then, out of nowhere, Rufus attacked the cat, and Amir rushed away to safety. A little while later, he returned to see if Rufus was ok. As Amir returned to the scene of the attack, he found Rufus dead with a terrible gash across his body. He dug a hole to bury Rufus, used a rock for his tombstone, and carved his name with a chisel-like bone.

***

A couple of months later, still sad about what had happened to Rufus, Amir had collected enough resources to make a raft and quickly went to work. Unfortunately, about this time, things were getting worse, for Amir found the body of his friend Joan on the shore. Since Amir was sad and had nothing else to do to finish his raft, he just went to sleep with the thought of sailing back to his wife.

Early the next morning, still sad, Amir prepared himself for his journey. He gathered as much food as he could transport on the raft, and coconuts so he would have something to drink on the trip. Before he set off, he visited Rufus one last time.

"Bye, Bud. I guess this is the last time I'll see you," Amir said sadly to Rufus's grave.

***

A few hours later, Amir got on his raft and set sail. "Hopefully she didn't forget about me," he said to himself. Amir looked down at the water and saw his reflection. He also saw dark clouds about ten miles away. "I have the worst luck," he said to himself as the waves started rolling in.

Within minutes, the waves were getting bigger, and then, suddenly, his raft flipped! "WOAH!" Amir screamed as he went flying into the air. SPLASH! he hit the water.

***

"What? Where am I?" Amir asked as he began regaining his vision.

"Sir," said Amir's doctor, "you've been in a coma for about nine months now."

"Honey!" his wife, Lucy, screamed.

"Amir, while you were in a coma, our son was born," Lucy said.

Once Amir was released from the hospital, he went home with his wife. Then, he asked her for a favor: "Do you want to adopt a dog?"

"Sure," Lucy responded. "What should we name him?"

"We should name him Rufus," Amir replied.

***

Amir, Lucy, and their son left the house and went to the animal shelter to find a dog. Amir finally found one that was hiding in the corner of his cage. He asked the owner about him and was told that he had been in the street.

He asked his wife, "What about this one?"

"He seems perfect," Lucy replied.

Polaroid

By Raina Stoll

Poli was a student at Heartpeak High School, which was a boarding school. She was pretty different from the other students at her school. Despite having small horns and a tail, she was very different in personality, being extremely nice but introverted. Almost every other student at her school was very social. Poli only had two friends, but she hadn't seen one of them in over five weeks.

Poli got up, dressed, and looked at a text that her friend Cam – short for Camila – had sent her: *Left something for you in your locker + come say hi b4 classes start, i'm at the entrance stairs.* Cam was one of Poli's only friends, since she was always too shy to talk to anyone else.

Poli texted back, *Ok, see you.* She grabbed her bag, her camera, and a photo of her and her friends, then walked out of her dorm.

***

The dorms were as underwhelming as they normally were in the morning. Poli always woke up early to avoid dealing with the other girls. She glanced around at all the doors, saw one slightly

117

open, and quieted her footsteps so she would not wake anyone up. She reached the stairs and started going down.

Poli walked out of the building and through the parking lot by the dorms, approaching Cam. Cam was sitting on the steps, listening to music on her phone; she noticed Poli and waved. "Hey, early bird," Cam said with a smile. She was your average 'punk skater girl.'

Poli responded, "Hi, Cam, you're up early." Cam was normally almost late because of how much she slept.

"Well," Cam started, "I had to do some things before you woke up, and I wanted to tell you 'Happy Birthday' before school started."

"Thanks, Cam. I honestly forgot that myself," Poli responded. She was turning eighteen and didn't care much about birthdays.

Cam said, "It's the job of best friends. Now go to your locker!"

Poli walked into the school building after waving goodbye to Cam. She calmly walked through the nearly empty hallways. There were teachers and janitors in the halls already, getting ready for the school day. She got to her locker. Inside was a box. There was also another smaller box beside it. Poli grabbed the smaller box and opened it; it was a container full of camera film. Poli was confused because her other camera had broken, so she had no way to use the film. Then, she opened the other box. It was the same kind of camera she had before, but it was clear Cam had decorated it, since there were stickers and drawings on it. Poli smiled and put the items in her bag and closed the locker.

The rest of the day was rather normal until Poli remembered she didn't have a photo for an assignment in her photography class. She went around looking for something interesting she could take a photo of until Cam approached her. Cam quickly put her hands on Poli's shoulders, making Poli jump. Then Cam spoke: "What are you doing?"

Poli responded, still kind of spooked, "Looking for something to take a picture of for an assignment."

With arms crossed, Cam suggested, "Why not take a picture of us together? We're on a lunch break; we can go somewhere."

Poli was interested in the idea. "Hmm, okay," she answered.

"Sweet," Cam said. "Follow me; I know a good place." They walked off campus to a flowery part of the forest. Cam practically threw Poli onto the ground, then laid down beside her.

"How'd you even find this place?" Poli questioned, calmly looking at the sky.

"I went on a little adventure yesterday to skip a test," Cam said with a smile. She was the type to do something like that, so Poli didn't question it.

"Okay, well, let's get the picture so we don't forget about it," Poli said.

Cam replied, "Okay," and moved closer to Poli. *Click.* They got a good picture. After hanging out for a bit, they both went back. When Poli was walking to her class, a photo fell out of her journal. The photo was of Kati, her friend who had gone missing. She had written on the photo. She picked it up, but looking at it hurt her head, so she dropped it. When she picked it up again, she blinked, and the first thing she saw was the flash of her old camera. *Click.*

Poli was confused, she looked around. She was outside the dorms, holding the camera that she had broken a week ago. She was very baffled, but more shocked than anything else, when she felt someone put a hand on her shoulder.

"Are you okay, Poli?" Kati asked, looking worried.

Poli just stared in shock. She eventually got the word out: "Kati?"

Kati looked slightly puzzled, "Yes? Poli, are you okay?"

Poli took a second, "What's going on?" she asked, extremely confused.

"We were going to get some breakfast with Cam," Kati said, "but I think we should get you to the nurse first. You're worrying me."

"What? Wait, what day is it?" Poli asked.

Kati answered, audibly and visibly concerned, "It's the 15th. Why?"

Poli seemed to realize what had happened. She quickly looked in her bag. The new camera was still there, as well as all of her other stuff, even the photo she had taken with Cam. Her head felt like it was being crushed for a second. She looked away while putting her hand on her head. She looked at the photo again, and when she blinked, *Click*. Another flash, and Cam was lying beside her. At this point, Poli was dumbfounded.

"Okay, what the heck is going on?" Poli said, sitting up.

"Huh?" Cam asked, taken aback by Poli's sudden change in mood.

Poli looked around, then thought for a second. She reached in her bag. Cam looked confused. She asked Poli, "What are you doing?"

"Just hold on," Poli said. She pulled out the picture she had just taken and the other from earlier. They were exactly the same.

What's going on? Poli asked herself, comparing them, trying to find a difference. Other than her writing on the first photo, they were the same. She didn't blink.

Cam looked very bewildered and asked, "What? How do you have two?" but Poli didn't answer. She ripped up the newer one, keeping the one with writing. She grabbed the photo of Kati from her bag and stared at it; she had no idea what was happening. She put the photo back and turned to Cam, who was extremely baffled.

"I have no idea what's going on," Poli stated.

Cam looked at the ripped photo, then at Poli. "What? What's going on?" Cam asked. She looked very concerned.

"I wish I knew," Poli answered. Her alarm went off. She was going to be late.

"Okay," Cam started, "you go to class, and we'll talk after. I'll come to your dorm, okay?"

Poli simply nodded and got up, still trying to figure out what was happening. When she eventually got to her photography class, she turned in the photo and sat down. A lot of things were happening around her. It was overwhelming. She glanced around the room, looking at all the pictures. She realized that nothing happened when she looked at them. She blinked, nothing. Blinked, nothing. Then, her gaze landed on a photo she had taken, and her head throbbed like it was being crushed by a sledgehammer. She looked away quickly.

Poli heard people approaching her. She looked up and saw the people she least wanted to see today: Bryson and Chloe. They had tormented her since her first day at the school; she ignored them a lot, though. They would do things like pull on her horns, yank her hair, push her, smash her head into lockers, make fun of her, and throw stuff at her. They had thrown her old camera at her before and it broke. She couldn't focus enough to ignore them today. She just looked at the table. Chloe grabbed Poli's camera and spoke. "Ooh, looks like the freak got a new camera."

Poli snatched it back. "Don't touch that!" she snapped. She was too annoyed by everything going on today to care about what she said.

Bryson grabbed Poli's hair and smashed her face on the desk, causing her nose to bleed. "Don't talk to her like that," he said firmly. Poli just wiped the blood away and looked at her camera, waiting for them to go away. Poli's nose was still bleeding when class started, and she was told to go to the nurse; she just went to the bathroom, instead. Poli looked at her reflection, then heard the bathroom door open.

"Poli?" Cam calmly said, walking over.

Poli didn't look at her, but said, "Hey, Cam."

"Hey," Cam responded, "you okay?" Cam hadn't seemed to notice her nose yet.

Poli didn't want to mention anything about Bryson and Chloe, so she didn't; but she had to say something, so she said, "Sure."

Cam noticed the blood and wiped it off, looking a little worried. She quickly spoke after grabbing some paper towels and starting to clean the blood. "What happened? Was it that Bryson guy? If it was, he's going to end up with more than just a bloody nose."

"I'm fine," Poli said; "calm down." She let Cam clean the wound. She was pretty calm about everything that had happened, with her injury, at least.

"Fine," Cam said, then took out a bandaid and put it on Poli's nose for her.

"Well, at least I can lie about going to the nurse now," Poli said, somewhat jokingly.

"Heh," Cam started, "you should head back, though. I'll meet you at your dorm, and you're going to tell me what the heck you freaked out about earlier, okay?"

Poli responded, "Okay. See you later." She walked out into the hallway and looked around. The hallways were as empty as they had been that morning. She wasn't used to being out of class, so she hurried to get back.

She sat down, not doing anything, not even listening to the assignment, just staring at the blood on the desk. She heard Chloe and Bryson whispering to each other. She ignored them. Poli always saw them as stereotypical bullies, which they were. She didn't know why they chose to torment her, of all people. Maybe they were desperate for a reaction, but she didn't know. She eventually wiped up the blood.

After class, tripping at the door, Poli headed to her dorm. Photography was her last class for the day, so she didn't have to worry about missing classes for this. When she got to her room, the door was already open. Poli had given Cam an extra key to her room.

Poli peeked into the room, Cam was lying on the bed, clearly waiting. "How long have you been in here?" Poli asked. Cam jumped slightly, not having noticed she was there.

Cam responded, "Since a few minutes ago." Poli walked over and sat down.

Poli sighed, then spoke, "I have no idea what's going on, and I don't know how to feel about it."

Cam took a second, just looking Poli over. Poli was visibly stressed; she was holding her bag tightly. Cam finally spoke. "Just explain what you know, P. I'm not going to push if you don't know."

Poli took a second, thinking. Then, she said, "I want to try something; then, I'll try to explain."

"Okay then, as long as I get an answer," Cam said. "What are you going to try?"

Poli took out her camera and pointed it at Cam. "Smile," she said. When Cam did, Poli took her picture. *Click*. She looked at the photo, her head starting to ache. Then, she laid out all of the photos in her bag.

Cam looked confused, but Poli spoke before she could ask anything. "Pick one."

Cam looked surprised, then laughed slightly. "What is this, a magic trick?" she said.

"You could say that," Poli said, then motioned to the photos. Cam pointed to the one of Kati.

"This one," she said. "What's this for?"

"Okay, now keep this photo of yourself. I'm going to take another, and I'll have two more photos if I'm right. One will be an exact copy of the one you picked, and another will be of me and Kati," Poli explained.

"Okay," Cam responded, confused, but determined to go along with her friend.

Poli took out her camera and took a picture of Cam holding the photo of herself and sitting with all the photos in front of her. She took the photo and shook it while putting her camera down. She put the photo of Cam in her bag and grabbed the photo of Kati and looked at it. Her headache continued, making her close her eyes. *Click.* Poli opened her eyes and saw Kati again. Poli didn't know how to react, but she calmed down and remembered what she had come to do. She walked closer to Kati.

"One more for good measure?" Poli said calmly.

Kati thought for a moment, then smiled as she spoke: "Sure."

Poli took another photo of her and Kati. She looked at it and then put it in her bag. She enjoyed a few more seconds with Kati, then took out the photo of Cam again. *Click.* Poli set her camera down, then reached into her bag. She set the two photos down. Cam was shocked.

"Woah, how did you do that?" Cam asked. Poli didn't really know how to answer her.

Poli responded, "I don't know, but it's weird. I feel like I'm moving through time. It's strange." Poli didn't really know what was going on.

Cam was too amazed to respond. Poli was looking at the photos, all of them in a line.

"Poli?" Cam said. "Your nose is bleeding again." Before Poli could respond, she passed out. When she woke up, Cam was standing over her, and the photo of Cam was burnt, along with the one Poli had recently taken with Kati. The fire alarm was going off.

"What was that about?" Cam asked, very confused.

Poli looked at her for a second, then responded, "What?"

Cam looked at her with a face of almost complete shock mixed with confusion. "What do you mean 'what'? You just set the photos on fire!"

Poli looked at Cam with groggy confusion. Cam looked back, very confused. Poli's nose was still bleeding. She realized she could barely see straight anymore as she passed out again. She was in a dark area, surrounded by photos. She looked around. It was pure darkness all around her, except for the photos and...who was that? Poli saw a figure with its back turned to her. She tried to talk to it, but no words came out. She got up and started walking closer to the figure. Right before she could touch it, she woke up.

Cam was at Poli's side. When she saw Poli was awake, she hugged her tightly. "Oh, are you okay? You scared the heck out of me!" Cam said. She was clearly very worried. Poli simply nodded.

"This is getting overwhelming for both of us," Poli said.

Cam spoke: "Yes, it is. We need a break." Cam helped Poli up, and they started walking out of the dorms. Then, something struck Poli. Her head was bruised. She looked at what it was, but before she could see it well, Cam picked it up and threw it at someone whom Poli didn't see, clearly harder than it had been thrown at Poli. It hit Chloe, the likely culprit. Cam was yelling at her, but Poli was zoned out and didn't hear it. She saw something in the forest edge by the dorms, a figure.

When Cam finished screaming at Chloe, she turned to see Poli walking towards the forest. She walked over and asked, "Poli, what are you doing?"

Poli jumped, startled, "I-I...uh, nothing."

"Uh," Cam started, "okay then."

Cam put her hand on Poli's back and started walking. Poli was looking back at the forest. The figure was gone. They were walking down the street calmly, not knowing what to say to each other. They were heading to their usual break spot, a small rundown park they had visited together since they were kids. Poli was looking around as they walked. She wanted to tell Cam about everything but didn't know how to say it.

Eventually, they reached the park. The only thing fully intact was the swing set. The rest was a pure mess, but they loved it there. Poli sat on a swing and looked at the contents of her bag, all the photos making her eyes hurt. Cam looked at her. "You okay?" she asked.

Poli looked up. "Huh?"

"Are you okay?" Cam said. "Your eyes dilated for a second there."

"What?" Poli asked, very confused. She felt slightly lightheaded when she glanced back at the photos. There wasn't a choice anymore; she had to tell Cam about it, about everything. She and Cam spoke for a bit, Poli explaining everything that had happened that day. Cam believed her since she had seen Poli do it. Cam was still processing everything when they started heading back. Poli tripped, and her photo container fell out of her bag. She looked at one of the photos and blinked from the fall. *Click.* Oh no, where is she now?

Poli struggled to adjust to the new setting. She felt a familiar hand on her shoulder. "Poli," Kati said, "are you okay? You look pale."

Poli just stared and thought to herself, "Oh no, I'm here again. What should I do? How do I handle this? Do I have my photos? I should've taken a photo at the park! I'm so stupid!" She simply nodded in response to Kati's question even though her head hurt. She put the camera in her bag and saw that the photos weren't there; she was stuck. Her camera was there, but there were no pictures. She decided just to try and wait it out.

Kati and Poli went to the diner where they were supposed to meet Cam on that day. *Time travel is weird...wait, what if I mess up something? I need those photos. I need to get back to present*

Cam. Is it present anymore? What about Kati? Could I figure out where she went? My head hurts... Poli passed out again and found herself back in the dark area, but there were more pictures. The figure was there, too. She looked at the pictures and saw every single picture she had ever taken, even the duplicates. She looked at the one she had taken before, of Cam. She needed to plan her next move carefully. She had to retrace her steps. She grabbed the photos she needed, put them in the bag, and looked at the figure, who was now looking at her. It was mostly a silhouette, but she could see the eyes. It looked...happy? Poli stood up after getting her photo of Cam, then started walking toward the figure. She held out her hand.

"Poli!? You're awake! Are you okay?" Kati was sitting beside her, clearly worried because Poli had just passed out.

Poli didn't respond; she just looked in her bag. The photos she had grabbed were there. She looked at the one of Cam and blinked. *Click.* Cam was sitting on the bed, holding the photo. Poli looked directly at her for a second, then reached into her bag and pulled out the pictures. She showed them to Cam. Cam was shocked.

"Woah, how did you do that?" she asked. Poli knew how to answer now, but she didn't want to risk changing anything, at least until she got back to where she was before.

Finally, she responded, "I don't know, but it's weird. I feel like I'm moving through time. It's strange." A lie, but she didn't want to risk messing with things.

Cam was too amazed to respond. Poli was looking at the photos, all of them in a line. She was getting really bad deja vu. She just had to retrace her steps.

"Poli?" Cam said. "Your nose is bleeding again." Before Poli could respond, she passed out. When she woke up, Cam was standing over her, and the photo of Cam was burnt, along with the one Poli had recently taken with Kati. The fire alarm was going off.

Oh right, Poli had forgotten about this part. "What was that about?" Cam asked, very confused.

Poli looked at her for a second, trying to remember what she had said before. "What?"

Cam looked at her with a face of almost complete shock mixed with confusion. "What do you mean 'what?' You just set the photos on fire!"

Poli just looked at Cam with fake groggy puzzlement. Cam looked back, very confused. Poli's nose was still bleeding. She could barely see straight anymore. She passed out again. She was back in the dark area. The figure was still looking at her. She got up and started walking towards it. She stopped and stared for a moment. The figure just stared back blankly. Poli reached out to it, but right before she could touch the figure, she woke up.

Cam was at Poli's side. When she saw that Poli was awake, she hugged her tightly. "Oh, are you okay? You scared the heck out of me!" she said. She was clearly very worried. Poli simply nodded.

"This is getting overwhelming for both of us," Poli said.

Cam spoke. "Yes, it is. We need a break." Cam helped Poli up, and they started walking out of the dorms. Then, something struck Poli. Her head was bruised. She looked at what it was, but again, before she could see it well, Cam picked it up and threw it at someone whom Poli didn't see, clearly harder than it had been thrown at Poli. It hit Chloe, the likely culprit. Cam was yelling at her, but Poli wasn't listening closely to what she was saying. She saw the figure in the forest edge by the dorms. "This is exactly like before except now I know what's happening. This is so weird. So, I think I walked towards it?" Poli thought to herself as she started walking.

When Cam was done screaming at Chloe, she turned to see Poli walking towards the forest. She walked over and asked, "Poli, what are you doing?"

Poli jumped, acting startled, "I-I...uh, nothing."

"Uh," Cam started, "okay then."

Cam put her hand on Poli's back and started walking. Poli was looking back at the forest, but the figure was gone. They were walking down the street calmly, not knowing what to say to each other. They were heading to their usual break spot, a small rundown park they had visited together as kids. Poli was looking around as they walked. She wanted just to skip to the part where she told Cam about everything.

Eventually, they reached the park. The only thing fully intact was the swing set. The rest was a pure mess, but they loved it there. Poli sat on a swing and looked at the things in her bag, all the photos making her eyes hurt. Cam looked at her. "You okay?" she asked.

Poli looked up, having forgotten about this part, then said, "Huh?"

"Are you okay?" Cam said. "Your eyes dilated for a second there."

"What?" Poli asked, very confused. She felt slightly lightheaded when she glanced back at the photos. Poli remembered it was time to tell Cam about everything. She and Cam spoke for a bit, explaining everything that had happened that day, excluding the 'retracing her steps' part. Cam believed her, since she had seen Poli do it. She was still processing everything when they started heading back. Poli avoided tripping this time, but Cam tripped, instead.

"Ouch," Cam said, sitting up.

Poli bent down. Cam's leggings were torn, and she had a scrape on her knee. Poli looked at it as she said, "You okay?" She cleaned up the blood from the scrape.

"Yeah," Cam said sarcastically, "my bleeding knee is amazing."

Poli chuckled, "Jeez, sorry! I wanted to check on you."

"How dare you care about me," Cam said jokingly. She laughed slightly. Poli helped Cam up, and they started walking. Poli tried to figure out how to tell Cam that she had to relive the same few hours of her life to get back to this point. Poli felt her nose bleeding. She wiped it away.

"So," Cam said, "what's it like, being able to control time?"

Poli looked at Cam for a second, then at the ground as she answered: "Stressful and confusing. I really don't know how to explain it other than that."

"Hmm, I would've thought it would be fun, being able to travel to any time you want," Cam said, nudging Poli slightly.

Poli looked at Cam and said, "Well, I can only travel to a time I took a picture."

"Oh, well, that's boring," Cam said, "but you've got to tell me about that weird dream place."

Poli spoke, not really knowing how to describe it: "It's dark there; I can barely see, but there are photos around me. There's always a figure there." She knew she had to tell Cam about the last few hours; she just didn't know how. She eventually gathered her words and said, "It's strange, that place confuses me, but it still got me back here."

"What's that mean?" Cam asked.

Poli took a second, then sighed, explaining everything she could. She explained how she got stuck with Kati for a bit, how she passed out and used the photos from the dream place to get back to Cam, and how she had to do exactly what she did all over again.

Cam took a second to process what Poli had said. "Wow, that's a lot."

"I want to find out what happened to Kati. Can you help?" Poli asked.

"Of course," Cam said, "but how can I help?"

Poli looked in her bag and pulled out her journal. She held it out to Cam as she spoke. "You keep track of what I find, okay?"

Cam took the book, thinking for a second, "Okay, but what if you get hurt?"

"I think my wounds stay where I get them. Mostly, at least," Poli said. They eventually returned to the dorms. Poli started cleaning up parts of her room as they talked, then cleared the board where she pinned her pictures and erased her whiteboard. "Okay, so if we're going to find Kati, I'm going to need photos and an idea about what I'm doing," Poli said.

"What's the photo closest to when we last saw her?" Cam asked. Poli looked at the photo she had. She took both the one of Kati and the one she showed Cam of her and Kati, which was still burned.

"It would be one of these, but if I go back to the first one, I'd have to try to remember everything I did so I wouldn't change

129

anything, which is in itself a hassle. But I don't think I can use the burnt one even if I wanted to," Poli explained.

"Just get as close as possible. If it means the same things, it couldn't possibly change much," Cam suggested.

Poli thought for a moment, then said, "Hmm, I've never actually tried that. Good idea."

Poli reached into her bag. She set the two cameras out. She thought for a moment, then threw her old one out. She left the one Cam had gifted her on the desk. "I'm going to need a spare if the one I took the picture with breaks. But this can stay here until I figure out what I'm doing," she said. She started writing on the whiteboard possible things she could do, then settled on one.

She said, "Okay, so I'm going to do what I did that day except that I'm going to follow Kati after she leaves the diner, since you didn't make it that day."

"Makes sense to me," Cam said. "Remember to take pictures before you come back, too," she added.

"Good idea," Poli said. She went up to Cam and took a picture. "And now I can get back."

Poli put the picture in her bag and looked at the board. She blinked at the photo. *Click*, and there she was, with Kati in front of her for what felt like the hundredth time.

Kati was smiling as she spoke. "Okay, let's get going."

Poli took a second to remember what she had said. "Okay," she quickly replied.

They started walking to the diner. Poli took in everything around them. *Jeez, why does this feel like so long ago? It was only a few weeks*, Poli thought. She kept walking, not realizing Kati had been talking to her. Luckily, that had happened before, but Poli couldn't remember why.

"Poli, are you even listening to me?" Kati asked in a jokingly stern tone.

Poli looked at her for a second, then said, "Maybe?" It was clear she hadn't even heard the question.

"You need to pay better attention to things, Poli," Kati said, nudging her.

They eventually reached the diner. Cam sent a text that she wasn't going to make it. Poli already knew this, but she had to keep up her act. Poli and Kati sat down, talking for a while. Then, Kati stood. "I need to go. See you tomorrow," Kati said. Poli knew it wasn't true. Still, she smiled and waved as Kati walked out. Poli followed her out. They went near the woods, and Poli heard rustling near Kati. She couldn't say anything, though.

Poli started feeling lightheaded, but she ignored it and kept following. She saw Kati get pulled into the forest. She quickly ran over and surreptitiously peeked in.

Kati was knocked out. She looked like she had been hit on the head with something. Someone was standing over Kati...wait, two people. A girl and a boy. They wore masks. The girl had a mask that didn't cover her brown hair. Poli took out her camera. *Click.* They noticed her. She put the picture in her bag and threw the camera at them, knowing that since she was already leaving, it wouldn't matter. She quickly looked at the picture she had taken with Cam so she could get back. *Click.* She looked at Cam for a second, then put the camera down.

Poli sat on her bed, taking out the photo she had taken. Cam looked at it and was shocked. "Jesus," she said.

"They heard me take the picture, so I've got to figure out what to do to avoid being seen," Poli explained.

Cam looked at Poli with shock. She spoke quickly. " Woah woah woah! You can't just move past this! What happened?"

"I honestly don't know," Poli explained. "I didn't see it."

Cam just stared at the photo in shock. "Okay then, we're just not going to try to figure this out?" Cam asked.

"I'm going to figure it out. That's why I'm planning to go back," Poli said. "I just need to know how to avoid being spotted when I go back."

"Okay then," Cam said.

Poli grabbed her camera and went to take a picture. Cam didn't want to be in the picture, so Poli took a picture of the board. She looked at the picture and blinked. *Click.* Poli quickly hid in the nearest bush in the forest, not even trying to look at what was in front of her. She heard rustling, then footsteps and something being dragged. She peeked out. They were walking away and dragging Kati. Poli followed silently, staying hidden while doing so.

They eventually got to a run-down shack by the playground Poli and Cam had visited. Poli snuck a picture, took out the photo of the board, and blinked. *Click.* She put the photo on the board, not saying anything. She looked at it, then looked at Cam, who was also looking at it. Cam had an unreadable expression on her face.

"We should look, shouldn't we?" Poli asked, looking at Cam.

She didn't respond for a second, but eventually said, "I don't think I'm ready."

Poli thought for a second, then reached for the camera. Cam grabbed her wrist.

"Maybe sit for a bit and think about this," Cam said, "What if we find something we don't want to see?"

Poli looked at Cam, a determined look in her eyes as she spoke. "I can handle it. I have to find out what happened to Kati."

Cam just looked at her with a hint of annoyance for a second, then sighed before saying, "Fine, just be careful."

Poli grabbed the camera and took a picture of the board again. She put the picture in her bag, looked at the one of the shack, and blinked. *Click.* Poli continued following and started looking for a way to peek in once the two dragged Kati in. She climbed up and looked in through a hole in the roof. Kati was tied up; she was awake now. She tried to take a picture but dropped the camera. She quickly pulled out the picture of the board and went back. *Click.* She set the camera down.

Poli looked at the photo of the shack again, not even bothering to look at or talk to Cam. *Click.* She went back up to where she was, looked in the hole, and held the camera tighter, getting a good picture of Kati and the two people. Before she could get the other photo out, she saw the female grab a metal bat. She flinched when she heard Kati get hit. She tried to move past it and get the other photo out. *Click.* She put the photo up. She looked directly at Cam and spoke, "I'm going to go look. I'll go alone if I have to."

Cam had the same unreadable expression. She just nodded. Poli walked to the door and started towards the playground. Then, she went to the shack. She pushed the door open. She saw Kati, but not how she wanted to. An overwhelming sense of dread came over Poli as she looked at Kati. Kati was very visibly beaten and bloody. Poli checked for a pulse. Nothing.

She heard footsteps. A very familiar voice spoke behind her: "I tried to stop you." Poli felt something hit her head. Then, she was in the dark room again and took the time to look around. All of the photos on the ground had been burnt. The figure was pointing to something, a photo. It was the one of Cam around the photos. The figure held out its hand. Poli went over and took it. She got a good look at the figure. The figure looked like her, but worse; she was missing an eye.

When Poli took the figure's hand, she remembered everything that had happened. This wasn't the first time Cam had tricked her. It made sense why 'a few weeks' felt so long ago now. "Destroy it," Poli heard the figure say. She took her hand away, and Poli could see she held all of the photos she had brought to that time. She blinked and saw Cam in awe, standing in front of her. She took out a lighter and set it on fire. Then, she was out again. She looked at all of the photos, the figure now gone. She woke up.

Cam was sitting over her, looking with a stolid expression. "Well, can't say I didn't try this time," she said. "Contrary to what you may believe, I don't want to hurt you. I just don't need you going back anymore." Poli just stared. She couldn't talk or move, just stare. Cam sighed as she spoke. "Don't look at me like that; I don't have a choice. I guess we've just got to do this again." Poli blacked out again.

Poli woke up in a cold sweat. She was in her dorm. What a nightmare! She was a student at Heartpeak High School, which was a boarding school. She was pretty different from the other students at her school. Despite having small horns and a tail, she was very different in personality, being extremely nice but introverted. Almost every other student at her school was very social. Poli only had two friends, but she hadn't seen one of them in over five weeks. She took out her phone.

All over again. It never ended. Poli never got out. She never figured out what Cam did. Time is confusing. We don't know if it can be manipulated, or if it ever ends. However, time can never be changed, no matter what anyone tries. Everything has to end, though...right?